LINE CHANGE

W.C. Mack

Cover by
Paul Perreault

Scholastic Canada Ltd.

Toronto New York London Auckland Sydney
Mexico City New Delhi Hong Kong Buenos Aires

Scholastic Canada Ltd.
604 King Street West, Toronto, Ontario M5V 1E1, Canada

Scholastic Inc.
557 Broadway, New York, NY 10012, USA

Scholastic Australia Pty Limited
PO Box 579, Gosford, NSW 2250, Australia

Scholastic New Zealand Limited
Private Bag 94407, Botany, Manukau 2163, New Zealand

Scholastic Children's Books
Euston House, 24 Eversholt Street, London NW1 1DB, UK

Library and Archives Canada Cataloguing in Publication
Mack, Winnie, 1972-
Line change / W.C. Mack.
ISBN 978-1-4431-0784-6
I. Title.
PS8625.A24L56 2011   jC813'.6   C2011-902457-8

6 5 4 3 2 1   Printed in Canada 121   11 12 13 14 15

For my hometown of Vancouver,
which will have its Stanley Cup someday.
And for Mike,
who will be thrilled when it does.

—W.C.M.

Chapter One

We only had three minutes left on the clock when things started to get serious. And they'd been pretty stinkin' serious already, thanks to the Thunder's left defenseman, who was grinding our guys into the boards every chance he got. I had no idea what his parents were thinking, but they'd named the kid *Adrian*. They should have been able to see what was coming and call him Tank.

Anyway, this monster had been knocking me around for the whole period, and I was getting pretty tired of the refs not calling it. Coach O'Neal was shouting from the bench, along with the rest of the team and our fans (well, families) in the stands.

I'd been personally introduced to the kid's elbow at least six times, but I didn't let that stop me. I was playing to win.

So I was pretty disappointed when Coach called me out.

I skated off the ice, passing our own hulking mass of muscle (and my Math tutor), Eddie Bosko, who high-fived me as he took over the right wing position.

"Nice job, Nugget," he said, with a growl like a grizzly.

"Thanks," I said, as I climbed onto the bench.

"That defenseman's a beast," Patrick Chen said, shaking his head from farther down.

"No doubt," I groaned. "Every time I had the puck, he had me."

"You played hard, son," Coach O'Neal said, patting me on the back. "That kid's at least twice your size and you gave him a run for the money."

I couldn't help thinking that if my stupid growth spurt would hurry up and happen, I wouldn't even be having the conversation.

Or any conversation about size.

"Man, I hope we can win this one," Patrick said as he pulled on his gloves, just in case Coach put him in.

I glanced past Patrick, where David "Bedhead" McCafferty was resting against the wall. He looked half-asleep, as usual.

It was too bad he never looked half-awake.

Seriously, who could relax during a hockey game? Especially when they were on the team!

I watched the game, wishing I was still in there. I'd had to accept the fact that Bosko and I were sharing right wing, but that didn't mean I liked it.

If I had my way, I'd play hockey every second of every day. It was my favourite thing to do, and I happened to be pretty awesome at it. If I wasn't playing, I was practising, and if I wasn't practising, I was either watching it on TV or reading about it.

Which reminded me that my copy of *Shoot! Volume 4* would be arriving at Chapters any day.

Yes!

Was hockey my life?

Definitely.

I leaned forward on the bench and watched the action on the ice.

We'd beaten Victoria before, but this time the game was too close to call.

They were a strong team, stuck with a weak uniform. While we looked dangerous in our black and red, the Thunder were drowning in purple and yellow. And it didn't matter that the L.A. Kings wore those colours a million years ago. There was nothing cool about purple and yellow.

I mean, come on.

But worse than Victoria's uniforms was their attitude. Just because they were from the biggest city on the island, they thought they were better than everyone else. They played rougher than they should.

Rougher than anyone should.

Hockey had rules for a reason. Seriously, it was a game, not a war.

I jumped to my feet as Eddie stole the puck from the Thunder's right defenseman. He hauled past the centre line, his skates scraping against the ice.

"Come on, Bosko!" I shouted, as I watched that nasty Tank move toward him.

That kid was fast, too.

Eddie kept the puck close as he skated toward the Thunder's goal, but within seconds Tank was right on his tail.

Our hometown crowd cheered as Eddie got closer to the net and I glanced up to see my parents and sister on their feet in the stands.

It was getting loud out there.

I wished the crowd was cheering for me. I wanted to be

the one getting ready for the best shot of the game, not my "partner."

"Take your time!" Coach O'Neal shouted. "Play smart, Bosko!"

We had less than two minutes left on the clock and we were still down a goal, so everybody was super tense.

I was hoping like crazy that Bosko could tie it up and send us into overtime. Then maybe I'd have a chance to get back out there.

I lived for overtime.

Eddie was eyeballing his target, preparing to take the shot. I knew he had perfect aim, and that Coach didn't need to tell him to take it slow. Bosko had patience, for sure.

"Shoot!" Kenny shouted. (His patience wasn't quite as developed.)

"Hard!" Patrick added, even louder.

I held my breath as Eddie pulled back his stick to whale on the puck. He had a killer slapshot (almost as good as mine), and I knew the Thunder's goalie didn't stand a chance. Bosko knew right where to put the puck, and I could already imagine it flying into the top of the net.

"Right in the cookie jar, Eddie!" my dad shouted from the stands.

I held my breath.

The crowd was going nuts.

The clock ticked behind its steel cage.

My heart bounced around in my chest like popcorn.

Bedhead McCafferty was . . . sleeping?

Never mind.

"Shoot, Bosko!" Patrick shouted, as we all watched the play.

It was going in, for sure. There was no doubt about it.

Of course, I *wanted* my teammate to score. But at the same time, Bosko was two ahead of me in a race for goals this season, and I was itching to take the lead. It was friendly competition, and a Cougars team win was more important than personal glory, but still. I wanted to be top dog.

"Shoot!" I shouted, loud enough to wake up McCafferty.

Well, almost.

Then it was like everything went into slow motion. The goalie was crouched in position, Bosko's blade was heading for the puck, and Tank was right on him . . . swinging his stick, high and fast!

Whoa!

Before my jaw even had a chance to drop, he hit Bosko right in the back!

The whole rink went quiet as our monster dropped to the ice and the puck slowly slid to a stop.

But the crowd was only silent for half a second before everybody went nuts. And I was right there with them.

"High-sticking!" I shouted to the ref, pointing at Tank.

He hit Bosko with the stick again, this time on the leg.

"And slashing!" I practically screamed.

Coach was shouting for a penalty, the rest of the bench were on their feet, and the fans were loudest of all.

"Blatant foul!" Coach O'Neal yelled. "Call it, ref!"

He was right about the blatant part. I'd never seen a kid be so obvious about trying to hurt another player. Sure, we all knew hockey was a rough sport, but playing the boards was one thing and slashing was something totally different.

The kid should have been thrown out of the game.

"Way out of line!" Tim yelled.

By the time the ref skated over to check on Bosko, our giant was already back on his feet.

Before anyone could stop him, he raced across the ice and shoved Tank.

The big guy went down. Hard.

"No," I groaned. The last thing we needed was a penalty.

The rest of the team backed away from Bosko and Tank, just like Coach taught us to do if it looked like there might be a fight. We weren't supposed to jump in. Ever.

Bosko made another move toward him.

"Come on, Eddie," Patrick murmured. "Keep your cool."

"Don't do it," I whispered.

The ref blew his whistle and called Bosko for charging.

"Their man was high-sticking *and* slashing," Coach shouted at him.

The ref shook his head. He hadn't seen it.

"You've got to be kidding," Coach shouted. "It was *blatant*."

The ref shrugged and directed Bosko off the ice.

Our gorilla would be out of the game for two full minutes.

Down one goal, with a minute and forty-three seconds left, and we handed the Thunder a power play?

Seriously. Handed it to them!

"Man, what'd he have to do that for?" Kenny sighed as we watched Bosko skate toward the box.

The second he stepped inside, Bosko said, "The kid slashed me and nobody called it."

Coach shot him a look. "It's not your job to settle scores, Bosko."

"But Coach, the ref is—"

"Calling the game."

He frowned. "But—"

"That's not how my team plays, Bosko."

"But—" Bosko tried again.

"Sit down and watch the game, son. We'll talk about this later."

I'd only seen Coach O'Neal look that mad and disappointed a couple of times in the three years he'd been my coach, and both times were when guys got too rough. He'd always taught us to play hard but fair and he had no patience for fighting.

At all.

I didn't look at Bosko. I couldn't believe he'd blown it for us.

Me and the rest of the bench tried to make up for our missing player with a whole lot of shouting and cheering.

But it didn't work.

The Thunder scored another goal with seventeen seconds left and we lost the game.

"Thanks a lot, Bosko," Kenny muttered as we all piled onto the ice to shake hands with Victoria and tell them "good game." Even though we didn't mean it.

Coach O'Neal saw Tank sneering at Bosko in line, so he shook his head and stepped out on the ice, heading straight for the Thunder's coach. If his scowl was anything to go by, it wasn't going to be pretty. Never mind the fact that he was wearing street shoes.

He only made it a few steps before his feet slipped out from under him. He flew up in the air, almost like a cartoon, but then landed hard on his butt.

"Oof!" Kenny said, wincing.

"Oof is right," I agreed, then skated over to him.

"Are you okay?" I asked, leaning in close as he rubbed his lower back.

It was pretty obvious from his scrunched-up face and groaning that he wasn't.

It didn't take long before there were parents out on the ice. Coach was answering questions with grunts, and when he finally did squeeze a word out, it was "Wow."

I had the feeling he wanted to say something a lot worse than that and when I saw the relieved looks on the parents' faces, I figured they must have been thinking the same thing.

"He's gonna need an ambulance," Mulligan said. He played Old Timers on Wednesday nights, and came to almost every Cougars game to cheer us on. "Anybody got a cell phone?"

My parents didn't, since they liked living in the Dark Ages, and my sister's was charging at home.

I was amazed she could even breathe without it.

"Ungh," Coach groaned, wincing from the pain.

"Is there a doctor in the house?" a voice boomed over the loudspeaker.

I'd never actually heard anyone say that before.

"Right here!" A man I didn't recognize stood up, then seemed to change his mind. "Well, I'm a veterinarian."

Coach groaned again and the man sat down, looking kind of sad that he wasn't a real doctor.

When Coach was carried off the ice on a stretcher, the rest of us just stood there.

"Nice work, Bosko," Colin said, rolling his eyes.

"If you have something to say to me, say it," Bosko growled.

"I just did," Colin muttered. "*Nice work*."

Bosko looked at the rest of us, and I'm sure he saw the same frustration in every guy's face that I did.

I wanted to say something in his defense, since he'd kind of become a friend while he was tutoring me in Math.

But at the same time, I knew I'd be the only one defending him, for something I didn't think he should have done in the first place. Charging? Come on.

I kept my mouth shut.

"You win some, you lose some," Dad said, quietly.

Like that helped.

"What a burn," Kenny sighed. "And now Coach is all messed up."

"What are we supposed to do?" Patrick asked, as the Thunder headed for the Visitors locker room, high-fiving all the way.

"Go home," I shrugged.

"No, I mean the team," Patrick said. "We've got two practices this week and we're up against Nanaimo on Saturday."

Nuts.

"Maybe we should cancel, until we know what's happening with Coach," Chris's mum said.

"Nah, we just need a fill-in," her husband told her.

"Who? You?" she asked, laughing.

"No . . . but somebody."

All I could hear for the next ten seconds was a bunch of fathers saying how busy they were.

Then I heard my dad's voice above the crowd.

"I'll do it."

And I grinned.

Chapter Two

On the way home from the rink, Mum didn't seem quite as excited about Dad taking over for Coach O'Neal as I was.

"Are you sure you have time for this, honey?" she asked. "You've had a pretty heavy workload lately. Can you really do this?"

"Cover a couple of practices?" Dad laughed. "Absolutely. It'll be fun."

I thought so, too. I'd always been proud of the fact that Dad was scouted by the Flames before I was born. When he got hit near the eye with a puck, it ended his career as a player, so he worked as a junior hockey ref for a while, which was cool, too. Not as cool as going pro, of course, but that wasn't his fault. (Except for the part about not wearing a helmet when he got hit. *That* was definitely his fault.)

Anyway, I knew Dad would make an awesome sub until Coach O'Neal came back. And thinking about my buddies seeing how much he knew about hockey made me look forward to practice even more than I usually did.

And that was saying something.

"This means getting up at five tomorrow, Gord," Mum said.

"Zero dark hundred," Dad nodded, then gave her a really goofy salute. "Got it."

"Okay, can you *please* not do stuff like that in public?" my sister Wendy groaned from the seat next to me. She was sixteen, and nothing on the planet was cool enough for her.

"Stuff like what?" Dad asked, glancing at her in the rearview mirror.

"I don't know. All of it," she sighed. "Talking and whatever."

Dad's eyebrows jumped. "Even talking? Geez, are you okay with the way I breathe?"

"Not when it's through your mouth," she said, looking out the window.

"Ouch!" Dad said, then turned to Mum and added, "You know, I used to be pretty hip."

"Seriously, Dad?" Wendy groaned. "No one even uses that word anymore."

"I know you were hip, honey," Mum said, reaching over to pat his knee. "But that was a long time ago."

"Double ouch!" Dad laughed.

"I think you're hip," I told him.

"Thank you, Nugget," he said, smiling at me in the rearview.

Sometimes us guys have to stick together.

* * *

When we got home, I went upstairs to have a hot shower and clean off all the sweat. It was amazing how gross me and my uniform could get after just one game.

When I dried off, I went to my room, where Mum was waiting for me with a bag from Chapters.

Shoot! Volume 4. It had to be.

"You picked it up!"

"Yesterday," she said.

"And you didn't tell me?" I couldn't believe she would hold out on me, especially when it was something so important. Something I'd been waiting for.

"You had Math homework to do."

Good call. I still did, as a matter of fact.

Even though I'd really needed the book back in October, when I was trying to win the PUCK Radio contest, I was still excited to read it.

"Awesome!" I said, when she handed me the bag.

I pulled out the book, and grinned when I saw the cover. It was a big picture of the NHL logo, made up of hundreds of tiny logos for every team in the league.

Sweet? Oh, yeah.

I started flipping through the pages. "I'm going to—"

"Read it later," Mum finished for me. "Homework first, honey."

"Nuts," I sighed as I closed the book and left it on my bed.

I knew from experience that Mum had the power to take the book away. And from a near-miss last month, I knew that my Math teacher, Mr. Holloway, had the power to take away my whole hockey season.

I wasn't about to test either one of them.

When Mum left me alone in my room, I looked at the walls covered with posters and all kinds of other hockey stuff. A picture of the room would have made a great cover for one of the "Shoot" books.

Actually, considering the amount of Jean Ducette stuff I had up on the walls, it might have made a better cover for a book about him.

A biography of a legend, just like the ones I had for Gretzky and Gordie Howe in my personal hockey library. Of course, the library only filled one bookshelf so far, but it was growing fast.

Aside from the books, the ultimate piece in my hockey collection was the jersey Ducette had signed for me when I met him at a Canucks game after winning the PUCK contest. I'd just missed my one big chance at a shot from centre ice and a big prize, but it didn't matter.

Jean Ducette made me forget I'd blown it.

Well, almost, anyway.

He was my absolute, number one hero.

I flopped on my bed and started flipping through the pages of my brand new hockey bible, but stopped.

Math had to come first. Period.

Otherwise Mum would not only take away the book, but stop me from watching the game that night, whether Kenny came over or not.

As much as I hated to do it, I cracked open my Math textbook instead. As usual, the homework assignment looked like hieroglyphics.

At least I had Eddie Bosko to help me pass, so I wasn't as doomed as I could have been. But I still seemed to be pretty doomed.

I took a deep breath and started the first question, wishing he was there to walk me through it. Everything made more sense when Bosko explained it, which was funny, because you'd think a genius would only explain stuff at genius level.

After about an hour I needed a break, so I checked out the Cougars schedule I'd tacked to my bulletin board, right next to my favourite picture of Jean Ducette.

The next month or so was looking good. Of course, we'd already lost to the Thunder, but next up was Nanaimo, who usually gave us a run for the money. Our record from last season showed we didn't finish that far ahead of them, so we'd definitely be putting some hustle into that game.

After Nanaimo came the Esquimalt Eagles, who were the lowest ranked team on the island. Hockey was never a joke, but playing the Eagles was pretty close to it.

Next were the Sooke Seagulls, whose goofy name didn't match how good they were. After us and Bosko's old Shoreline team, the Seagulls were probably the best team on the island.

We had our work cut out for us, and it would be weird if we went into games without Coach, but I knew Dad was going to be an awesome secret weapon.

* * *

That night, Kenny came over and we watched his Red Wings play the Blackhawks on TV, which was pretty cool.

But Kenny wasn't.

As usual, he was wearing all of his game night gear, including sweatpants, a T-shirt, hoodie and even a Red Wings tuque.

He was shiny with sweat about six minutes into the first period.

"You can take some of that off, you know," I told him.

"No way. It's my lucky gear."

Dad and I just shook our heads.

"Even the air freshener?" I asked, pointing at the logo hanging around his neck, totally reeking of cherries.

"Yup."

"You're taking it seriously," Dad said.

"I have to, Mr. McDonald," My buddy said, blowing on

his hands to cool them off before he put his Red Wings mitts back on. "If I'm missing one piece of my gear, they might lose."

"I see," Dad said, and I could tell he was trying not to laugh.

When Dad left to get drinks to go with the big bag of ripple chips I couldn't believe Mum had actually bought, Kenny said, "I wonder how long Coach is going to be out."

"I don't know," I said, shrugging.

"Because we've got some big games coming up."

"Yeah, Nanaimo this weekend, then Esquimalt and—"

"At least we aren't playing Shoreline for a while."

"We beat them last time," I reminded him.

Not that I was actually on the ice for the game. The Sharks were the biggest team in the league and Coach O'Neal always kept his tiniest player (me) on the bench for that one.

"Well, Nanaimo's a tough team."

"I know, Ken. I've been in the league for like, my whole life."

"Sure," he said, quietly. "It's just that it's going to be a big game."

"Duh," I told him, reaching for the chips and wishing Dad would hurry up with the drinks.

"And if Coach isn't back—"

"My dad will handle it," I told him.

"Can he?"

"Can he what?" I asked, turning to look at my friend, whose face was red. I couldn't tell if it was from being way overheated or from embarrassment. "Can he what?"

"You know . . . can he handle prepping us for that game?"

"Dude, he was almost in the NHL," I reminded him.

Kenny nodded, his face even redder. "I know, *almost*, but this is coaching."

"He was a ref for ten years."

"Yeah, and that's cool and everything, but I think coaching is . . . different."

I gave him a stare-down. Kenny wasn't really known for coming up with theories on his own. "*You* think, or *someone else* thinks?"

He winced. "Well, my dad said—"

"That he'd rather take over the team for now?" I asked, kind of in his face.

Mr. Cavanaugh was a hockey fan, but I was pretty sure he'd never actually played, even as a kid.

"No, because—"

"Because the only guy I heard offering to help us out was my dad."

Kenny definitely looked embarrassed. "I know."

"He's going to do an awesome job, I swear. And don't get all worked up about playing the Sharks and all that. Dad's only going to be running a practice or two and then Coach will be back."

Kenny nodded. "I know he'll be good. I'm sorry, Nugget. I shouldn't have said anything."

"It's okay," I told him, handing him the bowl of chips.

"Sometimes my dad's kind of a—"

"It's okay, Ken. We're cool."

Dad came back into the living room with Cokes for all three of us.

I was totally stunned that Mum had given in on that one. She was a nutritionist and she was as dedicated to health food as I was to hockey.

And that was saying something.

"What did I miss?" Dad asked.

"Nothing," I told him. "The commercials just ended."

As we sat and watched the game, I thought about what Kenny had said about coaching being different from playing or reffing. I wished his dad hadn't said anything.

Of course, Mr. Cavanaugh's opinion didn't matter, because I knew Dad was going to be the ultimate substitute coach. And everyone was going to see exactly how cool he was in a few short hours.

* * *

When my alarm clock went off at five the next morning, I guess I didn't hear it right away, so I woke up to the sound of Wendy pounding her fist against the wall between us and yelling at me to turn it off.

Oops.

Hers wasn't the kind of boat I wanted to rock at any time of day, but especially early in the morning. She was like an angry rhino at eight, and something even scarier before six.

I hit the "off" button and jumped out of bed, heading straight for the shower.

I ran into Dad in the hallway. His hair was crazy and he was rubbing his squinty eyes.

"Oh, you're up." His voice sounded dry and scratchy.

"Yup," I nodded.

"I was just coming to wake you."

"I'm awake," I said, nodding. "I have an alarm clock."

"Sure," Dad said, stretching as he yawned. "While you're in the shower, I might catch a couple more Z's."

Huh?

"Um . . . Mum usually makes breakfast while I'm in there."

His eyes bugged. "She does?"

"Yeah, because we have to leave by five-thirty."

"Right," he said, nodding. "Five-thirty. I'll get on it."

When he disappeared down the stairs, I turned to go into the bathroom. I glanced at my parents' bedroom door, kind of wishing Mum wasn't taking a turn sleeping in. I was used to practice mornings being just me and her.

We had a routine that really worked.

But maybe me and Dad would, too.

Once I was in the shower, I relaxed under the hot water and started thinking about how awesome it was going to be to have Dad as a coach, even if it was only for a few days. I hoped it would be longer than that because he would play me to my strengths, and I had the feeling I could score some serious goals.

Bosko and me had been splitting right wing down the middle, and we had a tight partnership, but an extra minute or two on the ice wouldn't hurt my stats a bit. Dad calling the shots would be a good opportunity for me to take over the lead.

I was already looking forward to leaving Bosko in the dust.

I towelled off, threw on my sweats and grabbed my school books before heading downstairs.

When I walked into the kitchen, Dad was sitting at the table with a cup of coffee, reading yesterday's paper.

I checked the counter for a toasted bagel or English muffin, but all I saw was a bowl of—

"Oatmeal," Dad said, grinning like it was a good thing.

"Oh," I said, carrying it over to the table and sitting down across from him.

"It sticks to the stomach," he said, flipping a page.

From what I could tell when I tried to lift my spoon, it stuck to everything, including itself. "Thanks, Dad."

"No problem."

I shoved the first mouthful in and realized I was going to need something to wash it down. When I got up to get some milk from the fridge, I saw the time on the microwave.

"Dad, it's quarter past."

"Mmm," he said, continuing to read.

"If you're going to have a shower . . . "

"Right," he said, folding the paper and drinking the last of his coffee in one gulp. "Be back in a flash."

He was pretty quick in the shower and I had just finished loading the dishwasher when he came downstairs.

"Awesome look," I said, happy to see him wearing his classic Nordiques jersey for practice. "Are you ready?"

"Absolutely," he said. "I just have to grab my skates."

He opened the door to the garage, which was a very bad sign. It was so jam-packed with stuff, I couldn't have found a *car* in there, if there'd actually been room for one.

I'd never even seen skates in there.

Ever.

"Do you know where they are?" I asked, glancing at the microwave.

Nuts.

We couldn't be late for his very first practice!

"Yeah, I think they're hanging by my workbench."

There was a workbench? Hidden under what?

While Dad tried to track down the skates, I grabbed my hockey bag from the mudroom. It was so heavy I could barely lift it. As I leaned against the kitchen counter and waited for him, I wondered why Mum hadn't made Dad get his stuff ready the night before.

I always had to.

Luckily, by the time Dad found his skates, we were only two minutes late leaving. He grabbed his keys and started for the door.

"Uh, Dad?" I asked. "Where's my lunch?"

"Your what?" he asked, turning the knob.

"My lunch. For school."

"I thought you were making it while I was in the shower."

"I thought you were making it while breakfast was cooking. That's what Mum does."

"She does?" he asked, sighing. "Look, let's just get you a school lunch today and—"

"Mum doesn't like me to—"

"Does Mum have to know everything?"

I smiled. "Maybe not." That was cool with me. Sometimes they had fries in the cafeteria, and that was way more exciting than a Mum lunch.

On the drive to the rink, it started to freak me out a bit that Dad hadn't even known where his skates were.

How long had it been since he'd played, or even been on the ice?

I was feeling a little nervous, for both of us.

But when he started talking about strategy and how he had some ideas he thought would really help the team, I knew it didn't matter if he hadn't skated for a while.

He might not have mastered the morning routine at home, but it was stupid of me to worry about the rink.

When it came to hockey, my dad knew exactly what he was doing.

Chapter Three

When we got to the rink, I hustled to the locker room to get into my gear while Dad headed for the ice.

On the way down the hallway, I could hear the guys goofing off, and as I got closer to the door, I knew they were going to razz me for getting there so late.

"Whoa, here he is," Jeff said, when I walked into the room.

"Uh-huh," I said, dropping my bag on the bench and opening it up.

"Sleep in much?" Patrick asked.

"I guess," I said, with a shrug. I didn't want to say that the holdup was Dad, tracking down his antique skates.

"Pretty cool that your dad's coaching today," Curtis said, as he headed for the door.

David and Patrick both nodded and said something about that being cool, but the only opinion I wanted to hear was Bosko's.

He didn't say a whole lot, but when he did, the guys listened. And since he'd seen my family in action during our eight million tutoring sessions, I really wanted him to be the guy to say that Dad would do an awesome job.

But he didn't say anything.

In fact, he finished lacing up his skates and followed Curtis out the door.

Kenny hung around while I was getting dressed.

"We're doing all our usual drills and stuff, right?" he asked, handing me my jersey once I had my shoulder pads on.

What kind of a question was that?

"It's still hockey, Ken. No matter who's coaching it."

"Cool," he said, smiling. "I don't like a lot of changes."

"Especially when it comes to your socks, right?" I laughed, punching him in the shoulder before I pulled the most awesome helmet on the planet out of my bag. Its red and black flames were the perfect match for my Cougars uniform. I still couldn't believe it was mine.

"Har dee har har," he said, punching me back. "So, are we heading out there, or what?"

"Let's roll," I said, beating him out the door.

The closer I got to the ice, the more excited I felt.

The absolute truth was that the Cougars had one of the best starting lineups in the league, and I loved playing with these guys.

I was the smallest kid on the team (and in the league, and in my grade, and on the planet, it sometimes felt like), but I was one of the fastest. What I lacked in height, I made up for in strength. And our giant, Bosko? He was a beast! Never mind the fact that his skills were almost as huge as his hulking body. He was quick, a killer stickhandler, and our other go-to guy (along with me). He'd left the Shoreline Sharks when he moved to Cutter Bay, and even though I wasn't a fan to start with, he'd kind of won me over.

And not because he wanted to, because the guy honestly didn't care what me or any of the guys thought.

Sometimes I wished I could be that way.

At left wing was Colin Bechter, who I'd played with since I was about five. He was a solid player and I could always count on him at game time.

At centre was Jeff McDaniel, who never failed to take possession when the puck was dropped. He was tight with Colin, but he got along with everybody. He was one of the strongest guys on the team, especially his breath, which was the worst on the island, mostly because of his beef jerky breakfasts.

Seriously gross.

Kenny Cavanaugh was my best friend on the team. He played defense with Patrick Chen. They were both nice guys and good players, but Kenny had really started to rock this season. He was finally getting to be as aggressive on the ice as he was when he watched his beloved Red Wings play on TV.

And that was saying something.

We also had the Watson triplets, who played left wing, centre and defense. Since no one could tell them apart, it's hard to say for sure which one played which position, but they were all pretty good. At least I *think* they all were.

Bedhead McCafferty filled in on defense when we needed him (and when he was awake).

Our weakest position was probably goal (and it showed — Chris Fullerton actually closed his eyes when we took shots at him during practice!). Our old goalie, Jason, moved to Calgary with his family, and that left the most gigantic team hole in Cougar history. We ended up rotating Chris and our benchwarmers through that position. Jeremy Simpson hated it and the other subs were Tim Shaw and Curtis Blank, who'd been on the team forever, but didn't play much. Tim's knee was sometimes messed up and Curtis wasn't much of an athlete. The two of them spent more time arguing over NHL stats than anything else.

* * *

When we got out on the rink, Dad was standing at centre ice.

"I think you all know I'm Nugget's dad and I'm filling in for Coach O'Neal." He held a whistle between his teeth while he was talking, which made him kind of hard to understand.

"When's he coming back?" Kenny asked.

"I'm not sure," Dad told him, letting the whistle drop out of his mouth. "I know he's in the hospital and they're figuring out how bad his back is."

"Will he be here for Saturday's game?" Kenny asked.

"He just said he didn't know," I whispered to him, and Kenny nodded.

"We'll find out soon enough," Dad told him. "If he isn't able to make the game, I'll coach."

"Cool," Jeff said. "Were you really one of the Flames, Mr. McDonald?"

"No," Dad said, raising his eyebrows when he looked at me.

"I didn't say that," I told him.

"I was *scouted* by the Flames, then had an accident and lost some vision."

"What kind of an accident?" Patrick asked.

"Can we just play?" I muttered to Kenny.

"I got hit with a puck and I wasn't wearing a helmet."

"What?" all the guys gasped at once.

"I wasn't playing when it happened," Dad explained. "I was taking a break on the ice."

"Did somebody do it on purpose?" Kenny asked.

Oh, brother.

"No," Dad sighed, and I could tell he was getting as tired of the questions as I was. "It was an *accident*. That's why it's always important to gear up and be aware of your surroundings."

"So if—" Kenny started, but I elbowed him.

"Now let's get down to business," Dad said.

He told us to skate a bunch of warm-up laps, which was exactly how Coach O'Neal always started practice.

Kenny looked relieved.

The team took off in one big herd, but some of us (like me) were faster skaters and pulled out ahead right away. Me and Bosko usually kept the same pace, and I'd gotten used to doing laps with him. He never said much, but that was okay. I needed to save my breath for more important things, like . . . breathing.

It was hard work, but it felt good to be pushing myself. Nothing sounded better than blades against the ice and a whole team of guys panting behind me. I counted off the laps as we went, hoping Dad wasn't going to go overboard.

"Let's pick it up!" he shouted, after a few minutes. "One more lap to go!"

Bosko and I both started gunning it, and I could feel the cold air freezing my lungs as I gasped for breath. Sometimes he beat me on the last lap, sometimes I beat him, but it was always a close finish.

"Nice work!" Dad called.

I gritted my teeth and skated even faster, because I

wanted Dad to see me beat all the other guys. Especially Bosko.

I wanted to be the best, even if it was only a drill.

And, with a burst of energy and determination, I was.

"Yes," I whispered, wanting to pump a victory fist in the air.

Instead, I bent to rest my hands on my knees and coasted for a few seconds, letting my heart slow down to normal.

"Nice speed," Eddie said, doing the same thing next to me. "Somebody had their Wheaties this morning."

"Thanks," I said, thinking of the oatmeal glued to my stomach.

When the rest of the guys finished the final lap, Dad started dividing us up into groups of three.

"Where are the cones?" Kenny whispered. "Coach usually puts cones out next."

"Relax," I told him.

"Each group get into a circle," Dad said.

"A circle?" Kenny whispered, like he didn't know what it was.

"Do you mean a triangle?" Jeff asked. "I mean, since there's three of us?"

"Sure," Dad nodded. "Circle, triangle, whatever you want to call it, just spread yourselves apart."

I was with Colin and McCafferty, who actually looked awake for a change.

Dad passed each group a puck. "We're going to work on cycling."

"Huh?" I heard Kenny ask.

"Cycling," Dad repeated. "I want one guy in each group to take the puck."

As soon as the words were out of his mouth, I'd snagged

ours.

"Now everybody start skating in a slow circle."

My group started skating and I heard Kenny say, "Coach doesn't do this."

Everybody ignored him and concentrated on what they were doing.

"When I blow the whistle, whoever has the puck needs to pass back to the guy behind him."

Before anyone could bug him with questions, he blew the whistle.

It was kind of a funny angle for passing, but I shot the puck back to Colin and we kept skating.

In a few seconds, Dad blew the whistle again, and Colin passed to Bedhead.

I saw that some of the groups had lost their pucks already. Dad waited until everyone was back on track before blowing the whistle again.

And again.

Faster.

And faster.

As we were running the drill, my group got better at handling those weird angles, and all of our passes were good.

"Nice," Bedhead said, when Colin slipped him the puck.

"The reason we're doing this is to get in the habit of passing when we don't have a good shot ourselves," Dad said. "Sharing the puck is a crucial part of winning."

He was right, of course. Everyone liked to be the guy who scored, but sometimes it was impossible to get a clean shot. I'd always looked for someone in front or to the side to pass to, but passing backward made way more sense.

I could tell that the other guys were liking it too.

Awesome.

When Dad blew the whistle in two short blasts to end the drill, he combined our groups, so we were two sets of six.

I checked Kenny out and he still looked a little worried.

Dad told us to make bigger circles and start passing the puck between us.

"It's just as important to be able to pass from a stationary position," he said.

"A what?" Jeff asked.

"Standing still," Bosko told him.

"Do we have to pass clockwise?" Patrick asked.

"No, you can pass to anyone at any time."

Dad blew the whistle and Jeff passed to Colin. On the next whistle, Colin passed to me, then me to Bosko, Bosko to Patrick, and we kept going for what seemed like forever.

"Nice stickhandling, Kenny," Dad said. "You too, McCafferty."

I waited for him to say my name, but he didn't.

Hmm.

Maybe he didn't want to be accused of playing favourites.

That was probably a good idea.

"Now, I want one of you to get in the middle of the circle and try to steal the puck."

"Keep-away," Jeff said, nodding.

"Passing under pressure," Dad corrected.

Nice one. "Passing under pressure" sounded way cooler.

"Bring it on," Colin said, moving into the middle of our circle.

Dad got us all started with the whistle, then it was fast and furious passing. We managed to keep the puck for

Colin's whole turn, then Dad called for us to trade guys. Jeff stole the puck from Patrick in about two seconds flat when he was in the middle.

My circle was pretty intense and I could hear the guys in the other group getting into it, too.

When it was my turn, I lunged at every guy who had the puck, but couldn't steal it away. It was driving me nuts! Dad blew his whistle and I was pretty disappointed in myself, especially when Bosko was up next. He snagged the puck as soon as Colin passed it to Kenny, then twice more during his turn.

Nuts!

To Kenny's obvious relief, when the pressure passing was over, Dad brought out the orange cones. He lined them up toward each goal, and since this was one of Coach's normal drills, we all knew what to do.

One after the other, we skated back and forth between the cones, and when we reached the end of the line, we took a shot on an empty net.

I made every shot but one.

Bosko never missed.

Of course, the guy had kind of become my friend, and he was still helping me a ton with Math, but that only made it more important for me to beat him on the ice.

After all, he seemed to be able to beat me everywhere else.

By the time we got through a set of line drills, skating as fast as we could to a cone marker, then back to the goal line, then out to a farther cone and back, and then even farther and back, I was dripping with sweat.

Line drills were one of the toughest things to do, and practically killed me every time, but I knew how much they helped my speed.

Dad blew the whistle and we met him at centre ice.

"Nice work, guys," he said, smiling. "We'll see you Wednesday morning."

Everybody froze, dead quiet.

What was he doing?

I glanced at the clock and when I saw that our time was up, my jaw dropped along with everyone else's.

"What about the scrimmage?" Kenny asked.

That was all it took for at least five other guys to start asking.

"We should be able to fit one in at Wednesday's practice," Dad said, as if that was totally acceptable.

He started scooping up orange cones.

"*Should?*" Patrick asked.

"Provided we get through everything else," Dad said, nodding.

"But—"

"Anyway, you really did a great job today and I'm already looking forward to next practice. See you then." He blew the whistle one last time and skated off the ice.

"What?" Kenny asked the rest of us. "What about the scrimmage? We *always* end with the scrimmage. It's the best part of practice!"

He was right, of course, but none of the other guys said a word.

I had the sinking feeling they were saving it for the locker room.

Chapter Four

I hung around on the ice for a couple of minutes, wondering what my teammates were going to say. I was as shocked about skipping the scrimmage as everyone else and I wished Dad had done things differently.

Of course, I couldn't avoid talking to the guys forever, so I took a deep breath and headed for the hallway. I could hear a bunch of voices in the locker room, and let out the breath before walking in.

Colin was in the middle of saying something, but he stopped when he saw me. In fact, all the guys turned and stared (except Bosko, who was doing his own thing, as usual).

I pulled my bag onto the bench and dug out my jeans and stuff for school, waiting for someone to say something.

Anything.

"What's the deal with your dad?"

Except that.

I looked at Colin and tried to figure out the best way to handle the situation.

"What do you mean?" I asked, hoping that playing dumb might work.

"Why didn't we get to scrimmage?" he asked.

I shrugged. "I guess the other stuff just took up all our time."

"But we're here to play hockey, not do stupid drills," Jeff said.

Nuts. I thought he'd be on my side.

But was I even on my side?

I was just as disappointed as everybody else about how practice ended. But saying so would be going against Dad, and I didn't want to do that.

"I know—" I started to say, but Bosko cut me off.

"Drills aren't stupid," he said quietly.

He could have whispered and the rest of the guys would have stopped to listen. After all, everybody respected Bosko, and not just because he was a giant.

"But we can't spend *all* our time on them," Colin argued.

"If they help our game, we can," Bosko said, then lifted his bag onto his shoulder and walked out of the locker room.

The guys all stood there for a second or two, probably trying to decide whether they should say Bosko was wrong.

Kenny glanced at me, then back at Colin, waiting to see who would say something.

Nobody did. Instead, we all just changed for school and packed our bags, like normal.

Whew.

That is, until I walked out of the locker room and stopped in the hallway to listen.

The first thing I heard was Colin saying, "Those drills were a joke."

"I thought they kind of helped," Kenny said, and I secretly thanked him.

"I don't think Nugget's dad knows what he's doing," Colin said.

I almost went back in there, but waited instead.

"Let's see how things go on Wednesday," Patrick said. "This was only his first practice. How was he supposed to know our routine?"

I smiled, thinking that was a cool thing to say. So, I had Patrick and Kenny on my side. That was good.

"All I'm saying is I hope Coach is back soon," Colin told them.

The rest of the guys kind of agreed, but that was okay. We all wanted Coach back. And Dad didn't want to *take over* the team, he was just helping out in a pinch.

Luckily, I had some time to set him straight before the next practice.

* * *

School went okay for me, but just like every Monday, it felt long. I had a quiz in Science, which wasn't too hard, but then I had Math class with Mr. Holloway.

I'd almost lost my chance to play hockey because of my Math grades, but thanks to Eddie Bosko and lots of studying, I'd managed to save my season.

The weird thing about Math was I'd thought once Eddie got me up to speed on the stuff that had been hard for me, I wouldn't have any more problems. I thought I'd be able to keep up with everybody else and never have Math trouble again.

But Mr. Holloway had moved onto new material.

Statistics.

At first I'd been all excited, because I thought he was

talking about the kind of statistics I loved. Sports statistics. And I was sure I'd ace the section.

But he wasn't talking about career goals or number of assists.

Instead, I was stuck trying to understand medians, means and modes, which made no sense at all.

When I sat in his class, I tried to concentrate and do my best, but always ended up wondering if Math was going to be just as hard or even harder for me all the way through school.

I had a long way to go, and even with Bosko's help, I worried that I wouldn't make it.

I glanced over my homework assignment as Carrie Tanaka walked from row to row, collecting papers for Mr. Holloway. When she came toward me, I saw her turn to smile at Bosko, but I couldn't see if he smiled back.

He had a huge crush on my sister, which was totally gross and weird, and I was hoping the fact that Carrie seemed to like him would make him forget about Wendy.

The yuck factor of girls couldn't even be measured.

I handed Carrie my homework and waited for Mr. Holloway to get started, hoping my brain wasn't about to get fried.

* * *

When I got home from school that afternoon, I had some of Mum's awesome banana bread and milk, then dumped my backpack in my room. I wasn't ready to do homework yet, since my brain was still sizzling from statistics, so I grabbed my stick and headed outside.

Nothing cleared my head like hockey.

There were wet leaves all over the ground, so I stuck a few of them to the side of the garage, to use as targets. Once

I found a tennis ball in the backyard, I got right to work, shooting at the leaves and waiting for Dad to get home.

He and I really needed to talk.

There was no way the guys would tolerate another practice without a scrimmage. No way.

After a few minutes, I'd warmed up nicely, and my shots were deadly. I seriously couldn't miss.

When Wendy came home, she rolled her eyes at me and went inside without even saying hello. As usual.

I kept shooting, even when she came outside again, holding the car keys.

"Mum said I can take you to the mall."

I shot the ball again and knocked a leaf to the ground. Perfect hit!

"Nugget," she said.

"I don't want to go to the mall."

She sighed. "Why not?"

"I'm practising."

"What for?" she asked, with her hands on her hips, starting to look mad. "You could hit those leaves in your sleep."

"Thank you." It was nice of her to notice.

"It wasn't a *compliment*, weirdo. You're totally obsessed."

"So?"

"So, I can't take the van unless you go with me."

"Why not?"

She rolled her eyes again. "Because Mum thinks if I'm driving alone, I'll use my phone."

They'd finally given up the fight and gotten her a cell phone for her birthday. And regretted it almost instantly.

I'd even heard them talking about cancelling her service if her grades slipped.

I never used the phone (unless I was winning the ultimate hockey trivia contest) and I couldn't imagine anyone having as much to talk about as Wendy did.

Seriously, her boyfriend Shane (Eddie Bosko's big brother) would drop her off at home and two seconds later she'd be calling him. Like she'd even had a chance to blink since they'd seen each other.

They slobbered all over each other, all the time. I didn't even want to think about it. Way too gross for me.

"I don't want to go," I told her.

"It'll take half an hour. I just want some lip gloss."

"You're going to drive all the way to the mall for lip gloss?"

Ever since she got her license, she'd been coming up with the dumbest excuses to drive. She even offered to pick up groceries for Mum or drop me off at school, just to get behind the wheel.

"Nugget," she warned.

"I'm waiting for Dad. Just leave your phone with Mum, so she knows you won't use it."

"What?" she gasped.

"Just—"

"I heard what you said, Nugget," she snapped, looking at me like I was nuts. "What if someone calls me?"

"They'll leave a message." It seemed simple enough.

She rolled her eyes. "You are such a tool."

"I'm not a—"

"There's no way I'm leaving without my phone," she said, storming back into the house. "Thanks a lot."

I took some more shots, checking the street behind me for Dad every couple of minutes.

When he finally pulled up and got out of the car, I followed him into the house, carrying my stick.

"How was school?" he asked.

"Not bad," I told him, even though Math had kind of ruined the rest of the day for me.

"Just not bad?" he asked, chuckling. "Well, anything would be a letdown after practice, right?" He held the door for me and smiled.

"Uh . . . sure."

"You know, I had a great time this morning," he said, leaving his briefcase by the door and hanging up his coat.

"Um, Dad—"

"So," Mum said, appearing in the kitchen doorway. "How did it go?"

"Terrific," he said. "It was so nice to be back on the ice. I'd almost forgotten how much I loved practice back in the day."

I tried to butt in. "Dad, the guys were—"

"Fantastic," he finished for me. "They really worked hard and it felt great to be giving them guidance."

"I'm glad to hear it," Mum said, smiling. "I was a bit worried, but it sounds like you were in your element."

"Definitely," Dad said, then looked at me. "The old man's got some tricks up his sleeve, eh, Nugget?"

"Yeah," I said, then cleared my throat, ready to say my piece. "The drills were good and everything, but the guys are kind of used to having a scrimmage at the end of practice."

"Sure," he said, loosening his tie and heading for the stairs. "Everyone loves a scrimmage."

"Right, and they love it at *every* practice. Since we didn't get to have one today—"

"We'll try to squeeze one in on Wednesday," he said,

climbing the stairs. "Like I told the guys already."

Squeeze one in?

That sounded even less likely than fitting one in, which I was sure he'd said that morning.

No, *squeezing* didn't sound good at all.

I sighed and when I turned to go into the kitchen, Mum was still standing in the doorway, watching me.

"Is everything okay?" she asked.

"Sure," I told her.

"The guys were happy with Dad coaching?"

"Uh-huh," I nodded. It was at least partly true.

"Good, because I just got off the phone with Mrs. O'Neal. Coach is going to need surgery."

"What?" I choked.

"He's probably out for a while."

Chapter Five

On Wednesday morning, for the first time in my entire life, I wasn't excited about practice. Sure, I was looking forward to getting out on the ice, since it was my favourite place on the whole planet, but I was feeling kind of weird about Dad coaching.

I just wanted the guys to like him and understand that there was a method to his madness. I didn't know exactly what that method was, but I had to believe he knew what he was doing.

At the same time, I wanted Dad to remember that Coach O'Neal had a system of his own, and that me and the guys were used to doing things a certain way.

An awesome way that already worked for us.

When my alarm went off, I stayed under the blankets for a couple of minutes. Just before I rolled out of bed, I decided that I'd have to be the one to keep things on track between Dad and the team. I'd step in when the guys were getting annoyed and I'd speak up when Dad was heading in the wrong direction.

I didn't have to choose a side or anything.

We were a team, and teams didn't have sides.

Once I was showered and dressed, I went downstairs, hoping Dad was a little more on the ball than he'd been on Monday morning.

The hoping paid off.

There were glasses of orange juice on the table, along with toasted bagels and every kind of spread Mum kept in the pantry.

"Morning," Dad said, as he bagged my sandwich for school.

"Morning," I said, sitting in my favourite chair.

I loaded up my bagel with peanut butter and honey, the ultimate combination of salty and sweet. My mouth was watering before I even took the first bite.

"I'm thinking plyometrics today," Dad said, joining me at the table with a cup of coffee.

"Plyo-what?" I asked, stopping the bagel halfway to my mouth.

"Strength and speed training," he explained.

"Cool," I nodded, lifting the bagel closer.

"Jumping rope, stairs—"

"What?" I asked, my mouth suddenly going dry.

What was he talking about?

"I was doing some online research last night and put together a nice set of exercises for the guys."

"Jumping rope?" I could barely say the words.

"Don't look so surprised. A lot of hockey training is done off the ice."

Not ours!

My brain was racing so fast I had to wait a second or two for my mouth to catch up. "Sure, during the off season, but—"

"During the season too."

"Dad," I said, feeling sick to my stomach. How was he going to convince the guys that we should spend our ice time jumping rope? And how was I supposed to convince them that he wasn't a lunatic? "I don't think the guys will be into that."

"Plyometrics? Nugget, I guarantee that every NHL team does this stuff."

"But Dad—"

"You won't believe the results."

And he probably wouldn't believe the reaction.

I practically dragged my gear to the van, and on the drive to the rink I barely said anything.

I mean, what could I say?

* * *

When I walked down the hallway toward the locker room, I heard Colin say, "Man, we better scrimmage today."

"Tell me about it," Jeff said. "What's the point of practising if we don't play?"

"Exactly," Colin said.

Oh, brother.

I walked into the room.

"Nugget." Colin glanced at me as he zipped up his bag. "Tell me you talked some sense into your dad."

All the other guys turned to stare at me (except for Bosko, who was lacing his skates).

"Uh—"

Before I could say anything, Dad was suddenly standing next to me. I didn't know he'd followed me in.

Had he heard Colin and Jeff?

"Skip the skates, guys," Dad said. "Meet me next to the rink in your running shoes."

He was gone in a flash, and when I turned around to face the guys, they all looked as stunned as I was.

"What's that about, Nugget?" Colin asked.

"Yeah," Kenny said, patting down his cowlick. "That didn't even make sense."

"Did he say *running shoes*?" Bedhead asked, still groggy from sleep.

"Uh, yeah." I dropped my bag on the bench. All I had to do was keep things running smoothly, and I could handle that. "He's got some really cool ideas for speed and strength training," I said, hoping that was enough.

And that it was true.

After all, I had some pretty serious doubts about the jump rope.

"But we're already fast," Colin said, shrugging.

"And strong," Jeff added.

"Well, there's always room for improvement," I said, opening my bag.

I put on all of my gear, except for the skates, and the whole time I was doing it nobody said a word.

"Ready?" I asked, when I'd finished re-tying my shoelaces.

"This is nuts," Colin said.

"It isn't, Col," I said, as firmly as I could. "I swear."

I led the team out toward the rink, and they were all walking at half speed or less, grunting and groaning the whole way.

When we reached Dad, I saw that he had cones spread out around the concession area.

"Okay, guys," he said, with a quick blast of the whistle. "It's time for some plyometrics."

"Some what?" Kenny asked.

"Plyometrics," Dad said.

All of the faces were still blank.

Every face but Eddie Bosko's, anyway.

"Cool," he said, shrugging as he walked over to a cone and stood next to it. "We used to do this stuff on the Sharks."

"You did?" Bedhead asked.

"Yeah. It really helps."

Yes! Thank you, Bosko!

A couple of the guys started whispering, and I hoped Bosko's opinion mattered as much as I thought it did.

When the whispering built to a kind of excited buzz, Dad's smile was huge, but only for a second before he got back to business with the whistle.

"Everybody stand next to a cone, just like Bosko."

We all scrambled to find places and waited for more.

"Do you think we'll scrimmage today?" Kenny whispered from next to me.

"Probably," I told him, crossing my fingers as I thought about "squeezing it in."

Dad got us to do a bunch of stretches, just like Coach always did, and I started to think things were going to be more normal than I expected.

But they weren't.

"Okay, I want you to jump over your cone," Dad said.

Kenny leaped into the air, like a hurdler, and landed with the cone behind him. He pumped a fist and hissed, "Yes!"

"I meant with both feet," Dad said.

"Huh?" Kenny asked, his jaw dropping. "At the same time?"

"I'll show you," Dad said. He stood in front of a cone with his knees bent. He took a breath and swung his whole body straight up, tucking his knees into his chest.

It looked . . . totally nuts.

"Seriously, Mr. McDonald?" Colin said.

"Yup," Dad said. "I want you boys to get some vertical height going, keeping your knees high."

It might have been crazy, but it looked easy enough.

I was wrong.

When I tried, I could only get halfway to the top of the cone.

"Maybe Nugget needs a mini-cone," Colin said, laughing.

"Nope," Dad said, shaking his head. "We're all in this together."

So much for favouritism.

"Every time I blow the whistle, you jump," Dad said.

And just like that, the torture began.

I watched for a few seconds, seeing Bedhead get some pretty good height while Kenny tripped and fell over.

I got started and by the fifth try, I was clearing the cone, but panting for breath. By the tenth whistle, my legs were already burning.

Why did we have to wear all of our gear for this?

By fifteen jumps, I could taste the sweat above my lip.

It was killing me, but I saw Bosko jumping smoothly, like he was born doing it. Sure, he was shiny with sweat too, but he was making it look easy.

That meant I had to step it up. With a grunt, I jumped again. And again. And again.

When we finally finished, after thirty jumps, Kenny and Jeff both lay down on the floor, gasping for breath.

Colin was doubled over and Patrick was wincing as he held the cramp in his side.

Bosko and I made eye contact and I could see that he was breathing almost as hard as I was.

"Okay, next up is the bench," Dad said, blowing his whistle again.

"Cool!" Kenny said, between gasps for air. "I'll get my skates."

"Not that bench," Dad said.

Nuts!

He pointed to the giant step where fans sat behind the goal. "That one."

He lined us up on top of the step, then explained that we were supposed to drop down to ground level, then jump back onto the step, with both feet.

"I can't jump anymore," Kenny whispered to me.

"It'll be fine," I told him, but I wasn't so sure. My legs were still shaking from round one.

"What does this have to do with hockey?" Jeff asked, in something dangerously close to a whine.

"Everything," Bosko said, quietly.

Most of the grumbling stopped. And so did the fun, as a matter of fact. Especially when the jump rope action started.

For the next forty-five minutes, the Cutter Bay Cougars did everything *but* play hockey.

And for the first time ever, I couldn't wait for practice to end.

Chapter Six

The last couple of days of the school week felt like two whole centuries.

Sure, we played floor hockey in gym, which was awesome, and yes, my oral report for English class went so well Mrs. Foster had tears in her eyes (or maybe an eyelash was stuck in there), but everything else was a drag.

We were still stuck on a Geography segment in Socials, and Math was seriously starting to hurt my brain.

"I think you're making this stuff seem harder than it is," Bosko said, as we sat down for our Friday afternoon tutoring session at my house.

He grabbed one of Mum's brownies from the heaping plate she'd left for us and took a big bite.

She didn't usually let me have more than a couple of treats, but when Bosko came over, she was all about the snacks.

I loved it.

"Why would I do that?" I asked, licking the warm icing off of mine.

Bosko stared at me. "That's what I'm asking you."

"Look, it *is* hard. All I want to do is pass. You already know that."

He shook his head as he chewed. "You should want to do more than just pass. You know you can do better."

"Not with statistics in the mix," I sighed.

"Okay, that's what I'm talking about," he said, through a mouthful of brownie. "You're psyching yourself out."

I picked up another brownie and ate it in three bites.

Bosko ate his in two.

I grabbed another one and shoved it into my mouth whole.

Only one bite! Take that!

Unfortunately, I practically choked on the brownie and was in the middle of a huge gulp of milk just as Wendy walked into the room.

Great.

Bosko stopped chewing and his mouth hung open, like he needed air.

Like a flounder.

"What are you doing here?" I asked.

Ever since Bosko fell in love with her and all that junk, we'd been scheduling our tutoring sessions at the library on the days she was home. That way, he wouldn't get distracted.

And I wouldn't puke.

"I live here, twerp," Wendy said, reaching for one of the brownies.

Bosko practically fell out of his chair trying to hand her a napkin.

This was the gorilla who slammed kids into the boards and took no prisoners?

I just shook my head.

Why couldn't he fall in love with Carrie Tanaka instead?

Or better yet, why couldn't he see that girls were a waste of time, like the rest of us?

"How are things going with Shane?" Bosko asked, trying to act like he didn't care that she was dating his brother.

"Good."

He closed his eyes for a second like he was in pain.

It was my turn to shake my head.

"I'm coming over to your place tonight," Wendy said. "We're watching a movie."

Bosko swallowed hard. "At my house?"

You'd think he'd just won a million dollars, not a night with a snotty teenager.

"Yeah. Shane asked me to give you a ride home when I go."

"You and me?" Bosko asked.

I thought the guy's heart might burst through his chest if he got any more excited.

"Yeah. Will you be ready to go in an hour?"

"We could go now, if you want to," Bosko said.

"Thanks," I told him. "I'm pretty sure we haven't even started our session yet."

Bosko glanced at me. "Right. Yeah, an hour would be cool."

Wendy grabbed one more brownie and walked up the stairs.

Bosko watched her every step of the way.

Enough, already.

"I know we've kind of been through this before, but you're wasting your time, Eddie."

"Maybe," he sighed. "Maybe not."

"Okay, since we're doing statistics, I'm going to tell you

that a twelve-year-old guy has no chance with a sixteen-year-old girl. Especially that one."

"You never know," he said, reaching for another brownie.

"What about Carrie Tanaka? She likes you."

He chewed slowly while he thought about it. "Yeah, and she's cute and everything, you know?"

Actually, I didn't know. None of them were "cute."

"Uh-huh," I lied.

"But it's just not the same."

I rolled my eyes. "Okay, so what *is* the same, is that Math is still killing me. Can we maybe get back to that, since the clock is ticking?"

I never thought I'd be begging Eddie Bosko to talk Math, but I couldn't take the stinkin' girl talk anymore.

We got down to business, and just like he always did, Bosko started to make sense of everything Mr. Holloway was talking about. Not perfect sense, but sense.

It was no surprise, considering my hulking hockey teammate was a bona fide Math champion. His "Meeting of the Math Minds" team had actually won at Nationals.

"Are you getting this?" he asked me, when our time was almost up.

"Yeah."

He gave me one of his classic stare-downs. "Don't just say yeah if you aren't."

"I'm not. I'm getting it."

"Cool," he said, patting his hair into place and glancing at the stairs.

Oh, brother.

Just then, Dad came in the front door, with his briefcase and a stack of magazines.

"Hey guys," he said, leaving the briefcase on the floor

and carrying the magazines over to us. "Check these out."

When he put the stack on the table, I saw that they weren't magazines at all. They were catalogues, packed with hockey training equipment.

"Sweet," Eddie said, flipping through the top one.

"There's some great gear out there for speed and strength training."

And maybe it should stay "out there."

I wanted to remind him that there was also something called a puck, which the Cougars liked to use every once in a while.

I cleared my throat. "Sure, Dad. But the thing is, a lot of the guys are starting to complain about not playing at practice."

"I think it's cool," Bosko said, still checking out the catalogue. "The plyometrics and all that."

"I think so too," Dad said, glancing at me. "They're very beneficial."

"I'm sure they are, but—" I tried to tell him, just as Wendy came downstairs.

"Ready?" she asked.

Bosko whipped around to check her out and almost knocked over his milk glass.

Geez, Louise.

"Sure!" he said, leaving me and Dad in the dust while he scrambled to get all of his books into his bag. "See you at the game," he called over his shoulder as he headed out the front door.

Wendy shrugged as she walked by us, but she was actually smiling, for once. I'd told her Bosko liked her, and I could tell she kind of enjoyed watching him drool over her.

She was twisted like that.

When Dad and I were alone, he sat down on the couch and invited me to join him.

"Big game tonight," he said. "Kenny coming over?"

"Yup. Ducette's been even more awesome than usual lately. The Bruins are toast," I said, with no doubt in my mind.

The Canucks were rocking and with my hero playing better than ever, the game would be in the bag.

I didn't have to wear all the gear, like Kenny did, because my Canucks didn't need luck. They were too good for that.

"So," Dad said, frowning a little. "The Cougars aren't too keen on the training, eh?"

I didn't know what to say, because I didn't want to hurt his feelings. At the same time, I wanted him to switch back to doing things the way Coach O'Neal did. The way we all did.

"I don't know," I shrugged. "It's just different, I guess."

"Different doesn't have to be bad, Nugget."

"I know."

"And they haven't tried for long enough to see what a difference the drills will make. I think it's a good idea to shake things up."

Couldn't he see that the only thing he'd really shaken up was me?

"Uh-huh," I sighed. Obviously, he was sticking with his plan, no matter what I said.

"Having a powwow?" Mum asked, coming in from the kitchen and flopping onto the recliner next to us.

"Just talking about the team's reaction to plyometrics," Dad said.

"Good?" Mum asked.

I shook my head slightly.

"Well," she continued, "Your dad knows what he's doing, Nugget."

"I know, it's just—"

"They'll get used to it," she said, like that was the end of it. "What do you guys think about chicken enchiladas for dinner?"

I looked at Dad and we both smiled.

It was that easy for me to ignore the fact that everything was starting to go haywire.

All it took to distract me was shredded chicken and perfectly melted cheese.

* * *

When Kenny came over that night, he brought a huge bag of Cheezies because he knew the ripple chips were a total fluke last time. If the package didn't say "whole grain" or "no preservatives" it rarely made it into Mum's grocery cart.

I could tell that even Dad was excited when he saw the bag.

"Kenny!" he said. "Good to see you. Let me grab a bowl for those."

"Uh, sure," Kenny said, as Dad took off with the Cheezies. When he was gone, Kenny asked, "So, have you talked to him about practice?"

"Kind of," I shrugged.

"That doesn't sound good," he said, settling at one end of the couch.

"Not tonight, okay?" I asked, ready to drop it.

"But—"

"*Kenny*," I warned, and he took the hint.

A couple of practices were bad enough. I hated to think

what would happen when the guys found out Coach O'Neal was having surgery.

I didn't even want to think about it.

By the time Dad got back with a full bowl, the game was about to start and his fingertips were already bright orange from whatever made Cheezies taste so good.

"Game on!" Kenny shouted as the NHL logo flashed onscreen.

The Canucks looked ready to rule the rink, and I almost felt sorry for those stinkin' Bruins.

Almost.

My favourite announcer, Dave Hodgkins, was calling the game, and even though I knew he was supposed to be un-biased, I also knew he loved the Canucks.

He and I were on the exact same page, especially when he started talking about Jean Ducette's phenomenal season.

The truth was, I was ready for a phenomenal season of my own, but it sure wasn't turning out that way.

Not wanting to think about it, I concentrated on the game.

When the puck was dropped, I watched Sean Masters scoop it up and pass it straight to my hero.

I couldn't help smiling as I stuffed my face with Cheezies and Ducette deked out three of the Bruins, heading straight for the net.

When he took the shot, it was beautiful.

"Yes!" I shouted, jumping off the couch. "Ducette is the man!"

"Cool your jets, Nugget," Dad said, laughing. "He's just getting started."

And Dad was right.

The guy was on fire!

It wasn't until the first period ended that I had a great idea. If the Cougars won, no one could complain about Dad's training methods. All I had to do was lead the team to victory, just like Ducette.

And I could do that.

Chapter Seven

I woke up on game day with an excited buzz in my ears, just like I always did.

The Nanaimo Penguins were about to get seriously creamed, courtesy of Nugget McDonald (and the rest of the Cougars, of course, but mostly me). I was going to play as hard as I could and take every possible shot for a win. I'd probably even pull ahead in my competition with Bosko.

Awesome.

And when we crushed Nanaimo, I couldn't wait for me and Dad to share the spotlight as the heroes of the day.

I could practically hear the crowd screaming as I scored another unbelievable goal. And I could see all the parents patting Dad on the back for coaching a team that couldn't lose.

I jumped out of bed and hit the shower, picturing the stunned look on the Penguin goalie's face when I came at him again, and again, and again.

It was going to be a game to remember.

Once I was out of the shower, I threw on my sweats, including my lucky Canucks hoodie, and I was ready to head to the rink.

Three hours early.

The game was scheduled for eleven, which meant no matter how much time I spent eating breakfast, there would still be hours to kill before I hit the ice.

I joined my parents at the kitchen table, surprised to see Dad scribbling notes on a pad of paper.

"What's that?" I asked, peeking over his shoulder while Mum put a plate of buckwheat pancakes on my placemat.

Bring on the maple syrup!

"Some new plays I'm working on," he said.

"For the Cougars?"

"Absolutely."

New plays?

I cleared my throat, ready to tell him that Coach never drew anything for us. He just told us what to do and we did it.

"Your dad's getting pretty serious about all of this," Mum said, smiling at me.

"Yeah," I said, deciding to keep quiet.

Maybe his notes would be a good thing.

Maybe.

I sat down and loaded my pancakes up with syrup. I loved every drop of that gooey, sweet, sticky deliciousness and could probably drink it straight from the bottle.

"That's enough, Nugget," Mum warned.

I stopped pouring, licked my fingers clean and dug in.

"I can't believe how much fun I'm having with this," Dad said.

"That's great, honey," Mum told him, pouring herself a cup of coffee.

"Of course, I know it's only been a couple of practices, but I can't help feeling that the Cougars have the makings of a championship team."

I stopped chewing. "Seriously?"

"Sure," Dad said, nodding. "You guys already managed to beat Shoreline once this year, and they're by far your toughest competition."

He was right about that.

"Yeah, and we beat them without Bosko or me," I pointed out. While I was sidelined for size, Bosko had been neck deep at Nationals, calculating Math stuff I couldn't even imagine (and didn't want to).

"Every season, that's the one team standing in your way."

"Uh-huh," I said, slowly chewing. "Sure, but they aren't the only team who beat us last year. Nanaimo won too. And so did Courtenay."

"Right," Dad said, nodding. "But those losses could have been prevented. Coach O'Neal is great, but he hasn't had you doing some of the drills that could take you over the top."

"Plyometrics," I said, once I'd swallowed my mouthful. The pancake kind of got stuck in my throat, despite all the syrup. I reached for my milk glass and took a big gulp.

"Exactly. The right training."

I took another bite and thought about what he was saying.

My master plan to dominate the ice was only about winning one game, but if Dad was ready to guide the Cougars to a championship victory for the first time ever, everyone would love him.

They'd probably put a statue of him in front of the rink.

"You really think all it'll take is plyometrics?" I asked, starting to get kind of excited about the whole thing.

Where would I put my championship trophy?

Would the Cougars have our picture in the paper?

"Plyometrics and some other new drills. Maybe some different configurations on the ice and—"

"Different what?" I asked.

"Move the players around," Mum explained, handing me a napkin.

"You mean, like, we play new positions?" I asked.

Dad just nodded.

I couldn't speak. I'd never even thought about switching the guys around. I'd been a right winger for my whole life.

Geez, I didn't want to end up playing defense or goalie or something.

How was I supposed to score?

"I think Bosko might do well at centre," Dad said circling something on his notepad.

Now *that* sounded good. I'd keep right wing, which I'd mastered, and Bosko would be stuck in a brand new slot.

I chewed faster, getting excited again.

It was genius!

We'd win games and I'd take the goal competition.

The doorbell rang just as I was imagining skating around the rink, holding the Island league trophy high above my head.

"I'll get it," I said, jumping up from the table and leaving my empty plate behind.

When I opened the door, Kenny was standing on the front step, holding a tennis ball and his stick.

"Wanna play?" he asked.

I looked at him like he was crazy. Of course I wanted to play. "Hold on."

I ran upstairs for some shoes, then back down, wincing as Wendy yelled at me to be quiet. She even said something about beauty sleep.

"Whatever," I muttered. If beauty was what she was after, she'd be sleeping for years.

No matter what Bosko thought.

"Ready?" Kenny asked from the doorway.

"Meet me in the driveway," I told him, zipping through the kitchen to grab my stick from the mudroom.

"Where's the fire?" Dad asked.

"Me and Kenny are going to play until we have to leave."

"Does he need a ride to the game?" Mum asked.

"I'll ask."

His family was . . . difficult at the games and that made me feel sorry for Kenny. After all, my family behaved pretty well when they came out to cheer us on.

Kenny's dad liked to yell at the refs.

But not as much as his grandma did.

When I got outside, Kenny had already pulled the net out from the side of the house. It had taken a pretty serious beating over the years, and some of the holes were big enough to let a bowling ball through, but that was okay.

"You need a ride to the game?" I asked.

Kenny glanced at me with relief. "If that's okay with your mum."

"She's the one who asked."

"Cool," he said, smiling. "So, you think we're gonna win today?" he asked, taking a shot.

I thought about Dad leading us straight to the championship. "No doubt," I told him.

"I don't know, Nugget. Nanaimo's pretty tough," he said, digging the ball out of the bushes with his stick.

"But they've only beaten us once in the last two seasons."

"Yeah, but . . . " he passed me the ball and didn't finish what he was saying.

"But what?"

"Nothing," he shrugged.

I lined up a shot and watched the ball fly right into the top corner of the net. "But what, Kenny?"

"I don't know. We're kind of off our game."

"Off our game? What are you talking about?"

"The guys were saying how no scrimmages at practice meant we wouldn't be, you know, warmed up for the game."

I snorted back a laugh. "It's only been two practices. If we've all forgotten how to play, we couldn't have been any good in the first place."

"But we're awesome!" Kenny argued.

"Yeah," I said, rolling my eyes at him. "That's the point, you goof. We'll be fine."

Better than fine, actually.

We were going to stomp on Nanaimo.

I would make sure of it.

* * *

When it was time to head for the rink, Wendy insisted on driving. If we'd taken Dad's car, that would have been fine, but I wasn't a big fan of her skills with the minivan.

Mostly because she didn't have any.

"How about picking a lane?" I asked, when she almost took us into oncoming traffic.

"How about zipping it, twerp?" she snapped, turning the

wheel so hard we almost ended up in a ditch instead.

Mum didn't say anything, but she had a white-knuckle death grip on her armrest.

"How about a little less chatter?" Dad said, wincing as the tires squealed on a corner. "And a little less speed."

"This is like Disneyland," Kenny whispered.

"Without the happiness," I told him, and we both laughed.

"Shut up, you guys," Wendy said, swerving as she shot us a look in the rear-view mirror.

"Eyes on the road," Mum said quietly.

"I *know*," Wendy growled.

"When are you getting your license?" Kenny asked.

Wendy's glare was back. "I already have it," she snapped.

"Holy smokes," Kenny whispered.

"That doesn't mean she'll keep it," I whispered back and we both snickered.

"I heard that, Nugget," Wendy growled.

"Everybody mind your own business and let's just get there in one piece," Dad said.

"What's that supposed to mean?" Wendy snapped. "I'm a perfectly good driver when I'm not being harassed."

"Just watch the road, honey," Mum told her, closing her eyes as Wendy swerved hard to miss a squirrel.

"If I die, you can have my rookie Viktor Slatov card," Kenny whispered.

"I'll probably die with you and I hate that guy," I whispered back.

"I hope your parents paid their insurance."

"My dad sells it, Kenny."

"Then he's a smart guy," he said, as his body slammed against me on another hard turn.

Of course he was.

My dad was about to lead the Cougars to the championship.

No doubt about it.

Chapter Eight

When Kenny and I got to the locker room, it had to be the gloomiest place on the planet. No one was talking and joking like they usually did. Instead, my whole team was dressed for the game, but acting like they were on their way to a funeral.

"What's the deal?" I asked, dropping my bag on the floor.

"My dad went and saw Coach at the hospital last night," Colin sighed.

"He's having surgery," Jeff groaned.

"I know," I told them, then wished I hadn't when they all turned to stare at me at once. "What?"

"You *knew*?" Patrick asked.

"Yeah, my mum told me the other day."

"Why didn't you tell us?" Colin demanded.

"I didn't have a chance."

"Whatever," Colin said, shaking his head, "So, now the next few games are a bust."

"No they aren't," I told them. "My dad's still going to coach."

"No offense, Nugget," Chris said. "But that's not exactly good news."

"More like the opposite," Jeff said.

"We're doomed," Colin said.

"Huh?" McCafferty grunted as he woke up for a second or two, then conked out again.

"No, we're not," I told them. "Dad has a plan and—"

"Dad has a plan?" Colin mocked. "I'm sure jumping up and down will stop the Penguins, Nugget."

"And Comox," Jeff added.

"And Shoreline," Kenny chimed in.

I turned to glare at him. He was supposed to be on my side. Dad's side.

Wait a second.

We were splitting into sides?

"You sound like a bunch of scared little girls," Eddie said, from the corner.

The guys turned toward him.

"But we aren't ready," Colin said.

"Aren't ready?" Bosko laughed. "We've all been playing hockey for our whole lives. Nothing's changed."

"But now that Coach is—" Chris started, but Bosko cut him off.

"Nothing's changed," Bosko said, this time a lot louder. Then he left the locker room. The chatter died down and I put on my gear. When I pulled on my lucky socks, I thought about how important it was to win.

The team had to see that Dad was the guy for the job, even if he didn't do things exactly like Coach O'Neal.

When I slipped into my shoulder pads, I knew it was time to play harder than ever before.

I pulled on my jersey and took a deep breath.

Then I grabbed my helmet and joined my team, ready to lead them to victory.

* * *

Nanaimo looked pretty threatening in their blue and black uniforms, but I could never figure out why they were the Penguins. I mean, why would anybody name a sport's team after something that *waddled*?

And would a penguin stand a chance against a cougar in the real world? No way. As far as I was concerned, in the lame name game, the Nanaimo Penguins were right up there with the Washington Capitals.

And that was saying something.

When the puck was dropped, we took possession right away and spent the first four minutes of the game close to the Penguins' net. I was taking one shot after another, but their goalie was surprisingly good. Even Colin was having trouble getting shots past him, until he finally managed to flick the puck between the goalie's legs.

"Yes!" I shouted, slapping him on the back.

Just a few seconds later, the Penguins' centre lined up a shot and blasted the puck toward Chris, who was stuck in goal. My whole body got tense as I watched the puck sail toward him, and all I could hope for was that his eyes were open.

Chris caught the puck in his right glove, and the home crowd cheered.

Whew!

"Nice save, Fullerton," Colin called out to him.

Chris nodded and got right back to business.

Patrick passed me the puck and I headed for the Penguins' goal, deking out both of their defensemen like it was nothing.

We were already on our way to a win. I could feel it all the way to my toes.

I'd spent the whole summer practising my slapshot and it was time to show it off. I raised my stick and swung hard, connecting right in the sweet spot.

The puck must have been going a hundred kilometres an hour, because it buzzed past the Penguins' goalie so fast, he didn't even twitch, let alone try to save it.

"Right on, Nugget!" Patrick shouted, patting my helmet.

"Sweet shot!" Colin added.

"I'm still up by one, Nugget," Bosko called from the bench.

"I know."

"*Up by one,*" he said again, with a grin.

He didn't have to be a jerk about it.

The competition was my idea, mostly because I thought I'd win. I wanted to be like Gretzky, the only guy to score more than two hundred goals in a season. And he did it four times!

But if two hundred was out of reach, I could aim for fifty.

Or forty.

Yeah, I'd probably be happy with forty.

But if Bosko won, I'd be sorry I ever suggested counting and competing.

Not that it mattered right that second, because the stomping of Nanaimo had begun.

* * *

During the second period, when Bosko was playing and I was on the bench, the game got a little tougher. The Penguins seemed to be getting more confident and taking more shots than they had at the beginning.

Chris Fullerton was handling them pretty well, but he did let a puck slip by.

Two to one wasn't enough of a lead against these guys, and I knew I had to get back out there.

"Put me back in, Dad," I said.

"Not yet, Nugget. Bosko's got it under control."

"But I can—"

"Not yet," Dad said, more firmly.

How was I supposed to score from the bench?

I sat down and watched as Kenny let one of the Penguins breeze past him and take a shot.

It went right in.

"What?" I shouted, jumping up. "Come on, Kenny!"

My pal shrugged at me, like he was sorry.

But sorry wasn't going to win the game.

And we *had* to win it. The guys had to believe in Dad's coaching.

"Dad, can't I just—"

"Not now, Nugget," he said, before I could finish.

Obviously, he didn't know I was about to light it up, so I waited as patiently as I could.

It turned out that wasn't very patiently.

Dad pulled Kenny off the ice and he joined me on the bench. He'd been a professional benchwarmer up until his awesome play earlier in the season and he was all excited about getting more game minutes than he used to.

"I just wish he'd put me back in," I muttered to Kenny,

"Me too," Kenny said.

"Because we both know I'm ready to rock out there, right?"

"Uh . . ."

"What?"

"I meant I wish he'd put *me* back in."

"Oh," I said, frowning.

"Because I can tear it up, too, Nugget."

"Yeah," I nodded. "Sure you can."

But not like I could.

Not even close.

Bosko scored two goals in the second period, while I gritted my teeth.

"He's ahead by three, eh?" Kenny asked.

Did he have to say it out loud?

I might have stunk at Math, but I could count goals, for crying out loud.

"Nugget, Kenny? You're in," Dad finally said, when I'd almost given up.

We both jumped off the bench while Dad pulled Patrick and Bosko out. It felt awesome to be back out on the ice and ready to play.

I was fired up!

In a matter of seconds, I had the puck and I swear my stickhandling could have been part of an instructional video. I moved that puck past my opponents, through their legs and around the back of the net faster than my teammates could say, "Wait up!"

I swerved around one side of the net and tried to find a shot, then slipped back behind when I couldn't. One of the Penguins tried to steal the puck, but I fought him off with a couple of elbow jabs and a quick slam against the boards.

I could hear the crowd getting rowdy, and I loved the sound of it. There was nothing better than knowing you had fans.

And man, did I have fans!

I whipped around the front of the net again and took another shot.

Score!

The goalie smacked his hand against his helmet and groaned.

I glanced at Bosko and smiled. It was catch up time.

"Nugget! Nugget! Nugget!" the crowd chanted, and I raised one arm in the air to let them know I could hear it.

The next thing I knew, Kenny stole the puck from one of the bigger Penguins and started hauling down the ice. I kept pace with him, ready for a pass.

When I got into position, just to the side of the net, one of the Penguin defensemen started giving me a hard time, poking me in the back with the heel of his stick.

"Back off," I told him.

"Make me, Peewee."

Enough with the size, already. "That's the best you can do?"

He poked me harder. "Whatever, you little jerk."

As soon as the words left the guy's mouth, Kenny whipped the puck to me. I spun around fast, slipping it right past the blade of the defenseman's stick.

Nice!

All I could see were Penguin uniforms, totally surrounding me, but I didn't care. I looked down at the puck and kept my eyes glued to it, trying to keep possession while hundreds of sticks (well, maybe two or three) tried to steal it away.

"I'm open," I heard Kenny shout, but there was no way I could pass.

I grunted and shoved my way through the bodies and suddenly, I had a clear shot.

Yes!

I flicked the puck into the air, level with the goalie's ribs, and he fell over trying to block it.

Goal!

"Nice job, Nugget!" Dad shouted, over the rest of the fans.

Only one behind Bosko!

Yes!

"Man, you're kicking butt," Kenny said, whacking me on the back.

"I know," I told him. "We're gonna win this."

"No doubt," he said, smiling.

The next thing I knew, Colin scored, and the crowd went nuts again.

I wondered if we were on the way to our highest-scoring game ever.

How cool would that be?

The Penguins seemed pretty discouraged, groaning when they lost the puck or missed a shot (and they missed a lot of them).

I almost felt bad for them, especially when I scored *again*.

Me and Bosko were all tied up, and I was loving it.

The Penguins' coach called a time-out and the Cougars all skated over to our box.

"Nice playing, Nugget," Bedhead said.

"You too," I told him. "Same goes for everybody."

We were in the middle of patting ourselves on the back and getting ready for the last four minutes of play when the Penguins' coach came over to talk to Dad.

"You wanna take it down a notch?" he asked.

"I'm sorry?" Dad said, looking confused.

"This is kids' *hockey*, not humiliation."

"I don't understand," Dad said, shaking his head.

I didn't either, and when I looked at the rest of the faces on my team, they looked as confused as I was.

"The high scoring," the coach said. "It's unsportsman-like."

"Unsports— . . . the boys are just playing the game," Dad said.

"My team didn't travel all the way here to be embarrassed."

"I didn't mean for them to—" Dad started to say.

"Your attitude stinks," he said, jabbing a finger right in Dad's face before he walked away.

When the ref blew the whistle, Dad didn't move.

"We're just playing the game," he said, quietly.

Chapter Nine

We ended up beating the Penguins by seven goals, which Dad seemed kind of sad about.

I wasn't sad at all.

A seven-goal win?

That was totally awesome!

That's what the game was all about, as far as I was concerned. Of course, I didn't play just so I could send another team home crying, but losing was part of hockey too. I was willing to bet that getting smoked by us meant Nanaimo would practise harder and play better next time.

"It was for their own good," I said, on the way home.

"Nugget," Dad sighed.

"You can't let that coach get to you, Dad," Wendy told him. "Nugget's right."

Somehow, knowing Wendy agreed with me made me doubt that.

"It's still a game, though," Dad told her. "It's supposed to be fun."

"It *was* fun," I told him. "It was the most fun game ever."

"I meant for both teams," he said.

"I had fun, too," Kenny told him. "If those kids can't handle losing, they shouldn't be playing hockey."

I high-fived him for that.

"Unsportsmanlike, he said," Dad said, quietly.

"Gord, let it go," Mum told him. "If the Cougars had won by twenty goals—"

"That would be sweet," I said, practically drooling at the thought.

"No," Mum corrected. "That would be excessive. That would be the time you relaxed and let some of the kids who don't play as much get out there."

"I think it would be the time you go for thirty goals," I whispered to Kenny. "Like an all-time high. *Guinness Book of World Records* style."

"Watch out for that Volvo, Wendy," Dad said, grabbing the door handle. "That was close."

"Can you guys relax?" Wendy snapped. "Just let me drive, okay? I know what I'm doing."

"But not which lane she's doing it in," Kenny whispered and I laughed.

"Shut up, you two," she said, glaring in the rear-view mirror.

"The whole idea used to be play to win," Dad said, shaking his head. "It wasn't about hurt feelings."

"It still is play to win," I told him. "The Penguins were just mad they weren't the ones doing it."

"Back in my day, the coach didn't have to think about the other team's feelings," Dad said, quietly.

"Well, your day was like a thousand years ago," Wendy told him.

"Honey, losing is an important part of sports," Mum said.

"Just like fibre is an important part of our diet," I said.

She shot me a look. "So is confidence and self-esteem. I swear, Gord, if I thought you'd done anything wrong or should have coached differently, I'd tell you."

"Thanks, honey," he said, turning to smile at her. When he turned back, he asked, very calmly, "You see that pedestrian, right Wendy?"

"Duh," she said, rolling her eyes.

"I'm talking about the one on your left," Dad said, gripping his seat.

"What?" Wendy asked, eyes bugging. "Oh!"

The minivan swerved hard.

"Slow down!" Mum said.

"I am!"

"Slower!" Mum shouted.

Wendy slammed on the brakes and the van screeched to a stop. She unbuckled her seatbelt. "I can't handle this anymore."

"*You* can't?" I gasped, trying to catch my breath. My seatbelt was going to leave a bright red mark across my chest, like the sash from a freakin' beauty pageant!

Kenny looked ready to hurl.

"You can't just stop in the middle of the road," Mum said. "Gord, do something."

Dad was already out of the car, waving for people to stop honking their horns. He walked around the back of the van and Wendy came around the front to take over the passenger seat.

"I can't believe you guys," she muttered, as she buckled up. "You get all stressed and that totally freaks me out."

"You have to be in control when you're driving," Dad told her. "That includes control of the car and your emotions."

"She's a teenager," I reminded him. "Her hormones are going crazy and—"

"Zip it, Nugget," Wendy snapped. "Look, I drive better when I'm by myself, okay?"

"Yeah, right," Kenny whispered.

* * *

That night, the Canucks were playing an away game against the Avalanche and I was in charge of snacks.

Just before game time, I headed for the kitchen, where I pulled out bowls and glasses for me and Dad. Then I started digging in the pantry for whatever could pass for chips and treats.

The worst thing about Mum being a nutritionist was that she thought "snack" and "fruit" were the same thing.

"Are things going okay at the rink?" Mum asked.

"Uh-huh," I told her.

"Care to elaborate?" she asked. When I looked confused, she said, "You know how I feel about one-word answers."

I found the Tupperware container of carob cookies, which were actually pretty good, and some pita chips. If we had dip in the fridge, I'd be in business.

"I think everything's fine," I told her. "Now that we've won a game, everything will calm down."

She raised an eyebrow, which was her best interrogation technique. "What needed to calm down?"

"Oh, you know. The guys didn't like some of the changes to practice."

"Well, the guys aren't in charge," she said.

"I know, Mum. You asked, and I'm telling you." I lined up the cookies on a plate. "Are you watching the game with us?"

"No, I'm working on a diabetic meal plan for a new client," she said, glancing at me and frowning. "And I'll be working on one for you if you don't put back at least half of those cookies."

"But they're the healthy kind," I reminded her. "Made by your own loving hands."

"That doesn't mean they should be eaten by the dozen." She shook her head. "I'm serious, Nugget. Cut that down by half."

"Fine," I sighed, putting most of them back in the Tupperware. "Do we have any popcorn?"

"I see pita chips on the counter."

"I know, but—"

"It's in the pantry," she sighed. "But you are not melting butter."

"What?" I choked. "We're supposed to eat it plain?"

"You pop it and I'll season it for you."

"Season it? Mum, popcorn is made to be soaked in butter."

"And people are made to live past twenty-five."

"Whatever," I groaned.

When I grew up and had a place of my own, the whole pantry, fridge and even my closet would be jam-packed with junk food. I already had a lot of years to make up for in missed Doritos and ice cream.

Once I had all my snacks perfectly organized and heard Dad turn on the TV, I remembered something super important.

We'd blown past the first of the month without a height measurement.

"Wait, let me get the ruler," I told Mum, digging through the junk drawer.

She knew what I was doing right away.

"Why don't we just wait until next month?" she asked hopefully.

"No way!"

In the last couple of months, I hadn't even grown a centimetre, and I was pretty sick of waiting. Mum kept promising a growth spurt, but I was starting to doubt her, especially when I looked at the pencil marks next to the fridge, all stuck around the same place.

I stood against the wall and pushed my shoulder blades back.

"Fine," she said, sighing as she reached for the ruler and the pencil.

I stood as still as I could while she measured. "I don't think this kind of obsession is healthy, honey," she said quietly.

"Neither is being the size of a four-year-old in grade six."

"You're bigger than a four-year-old."

"Is that supposed to make me feel better?"

"You're the one who brought it up," she said.

I closed my eyes and held my breath while I waited for her to finish.

"Not bad," she said, once she'd marked the spot.

I spun around but didn't open my eyes until I was facing the wall. The new mark was higher than the last one, but not by much.

Great.

"A pinch," I told her, frowning.

"A smidge," she said, ruffling my hair. "You'll get there."

"When I'm eighty?"

"Look at your sister," Mum said, with a shrug.

Sure, Wendy was hoping she wouldn't hit six feet before she graduated from high school, but she'd never had to wait for a growth spurt. She'd been tall all along.

It wasn't fair.

At that moment, the doorbell rang and Wendy ran to answer it, which meant it had to be Shane. As I carried my tray of snacks into the living room, I ignored the slurpy kissing noises.

Gross.

"Ready?" Dad asked, as I put the tray on the coffee table and flopped onto my favourite side of the couch.

"Definitely," I told him, grinning. I loved watching games with Dad because we both got totally into it.

Sometimes we cheered, sometimes we screamed, and sometimes we even ended up rolling on the floor and kicking our feet.

What can I say? We were fans.

Just as I grabbed a handful of popcorn, Wendy and Shane walked in.

"Hockey game, Mr. McDonald?" Shane asked.

Duh.

"We're about to destroy Colorado," I told him.

"How are things going with the coaching?" Shane asked, totally ignoring me.

Bosko told me he ignored almost everybody.

Except Wendy.

"Pretty well, I think," Dad said.

"Cool," Shane said, nodding. "My little brother's digging it." I almost laughed, amazed to hear anyone call the only kid in grade six with a mustache "little."

"Do you two want to join us?" Dad asked, starting to make room on the couch.

"No way," Wendy said, rolling her eyes.

"Thanks, anyway," Shane said. "I'm not much of a hockey fan."

"That's right," Dad nodded. "You're a rugby guy."

"No pads," Shane shrugged, like that made him some kind of a superhero. "No helmets."

"No brains," I muttered.

"What did you just say?" Wendy asked.

I could tell by the look in her eyes that if she couldn't pin me right then, she'd definitely do it later.

"Nothing," I said, shoving a handful of popcorn past my lips.

Mum might have thought snacks would be the death of me, but that night a mouthful probably saved my life.

Chapter Ten

On Monday morning, I woke up for practice with a huge smile. Our big win guaranteed that my teammates would be on board with Dad's coaching, my own four goals were a career high for me, and I was ahead of Bosko by a goal.

Nugget McDonald takes the lead!

Awesome?

Oh, yeah.

I sang to myself in the shower, but very quietly, so I wouldn't wake Wendy up. I didn't need a perfectly good morning ruined by the crabbiest teenager on the planet.

As I dried off and got dressed, I cut the singing back to humming.

Practice was going to be just like I imagined, with me and Dad as joint heroes.

Never mind the fact that all of my homework was done. I'd understood every bit of my Math assignment (except for three of the questions, but still) and I'd finished the book we were reading for English class a whole week early.

Mrs. Foster had continued to freak out every time I

raised my hand to answer her questions in class. It should have gotten old by then, but she was still surprised that I'd turned my study habits around.

I was amazed how much I liked reading now, and not just hockey books. The one we'd been reading in class was about a kid who had to choose between his two best friends, who were going in totally different directions.

When I thought about how things had been going between Dad and the Cougars, I could totally "identify," as Mrs. Foster would say. But luckily I wasn't like the kid in the book. Thanks to the weekend win, I didn't have to choose sides.

We were all on the same team again.

I joined Dad in the kitchen, where a plate of toast was waiting for me.

"Hot diggity," I said, smothering a slice with peanut butter.

"How did you sleep?" he asked, taking a sip of his coffee.

"Good. I had a dream that me and Jean Ducette won the Stanley Cup."

Dad laughed. "I wouldn't have wanted to wake up from that one."

"Me neither," I said, taking a bite of my toast. It was kind of burnt, but the peanut butter covered up the taste a bit. "It's easier to get up on practice days, though."

Dad loaded the dishwasher and wiped the counters while I ate.

"Did you already have breakfast?" I asked him.

"I'm not feeling hungry," he said.

For the first time, I noticed he had bags under his eyes.

"How did *you* sleep?" I asked him.

"I don't know," he said, with a shrug. "I tossed and turned a bit, thinking about what that coach said."

"Geez, Dad, you can't let it get to you. The guy was just mad his team was losing."

Losing big.

No, make that *huge*.

"I know, but—"

"Seriously, Dad. He wanted to psych you out, and it worked." I shoved the last bite of toast into my mouth and chased it down with a huge gulp of milk. I rinsed off my dishes and put them in the dishwasher, then headed for the mudroom.

"Don't worry about your gear," Dad said.

"Thanks," I said, figuring he must have loaded it into the van already. "I could have carried it out, Dad."

"It's still in the mudroom," he said. "I meant don't worry about bringing it."

"What are you talking about?" I asked, trying to ignore the sinking feeling in my stomach.

"You won't need it today."

I stared at him. "Dad, we're leaving for practice in like, two minutes."

"I know," he said, laughing. "Are you awake yet, Nugget? I'm saying you don't need gear for today's practice. Just wear what you have on and make sure you grab some running shoes."

I couldn't be hearing him right.

"What about my stick?"

"Leave it."

Leave it?

My stick? The tool of my trade?

He disappeared out to the garage and I was left standing there, with my stomach sinking even deeper.

How were we supposed to have a hockey practice with

no pads, no skates, and no sticks?

When he came back, I knew I had to say something.

"Dad, I know you have a plan and everything, but the guys aren't going to go along with this."

He laughed. "Of course they are. Do you think they will have forgotten about Saturday's win already?"

"Um, I'm pretty sure we would have won that game no matter what."

He raised an eyebrow at me. "I'm just going to do what I can to keep the streak going, Nugget."

"Seriously, Dad. A hockey practice without gear is like . . . *not* a hockey practice."

"Trust me, son," he said.

And I wanted to.

But the guys wouldn't trust him at all.

* * *

It turned out that Mum got the phone tree started the night before, calling Mrs. Bechter to tell her no one needed gear for practice. She called Mrs. Cavanaugh, who called Mrs. Chen, and on it went down the alphabetical list until everyone knew we wouldn't be on the ice the next morning.

And that meant instead of dropping the guys off and leaving, a couple of the mums hung around to see what was going on.

Instead of heading straight for the locker room, I listened in from the hallway.

"The boys will be running," Dad explained.

"Running where?" Mrs. Simpson asked.

"Out there," Dad said, pointing outside. "The fair streets of Cutter Bay."

"But they're meant to be skating," Mrs. Fullerton said. "This is hockey practice, not track and field."

"It's all part of training," Dad said, smiling. "These boys are great on the ice. Their puck handling is exceptional, they shoot well, and their speed is great. Doing some work off the ice will only make them stronger on it."

"Okay," Mrs. Simpson said, sounding doubtful. "But my husband wanted me to point out that we're paying for ice time."

"And that isn't cheap," Mrs. Fullerton added.

"You're absolutely right," Dad agreed, nodding. "I traded our time with another team for today. We'll get an extra hour of ice at the next practice. It'll be an early morning on Wednesday, but we'll get our time in."

Two hours on the ice? Cool! I couldn't help grinning. Maybe Dad had a good plan after all.

"I see," Mrs. Simpson said, glancing at Mrs. Fullerton, who nodded. "Well, that sounds perfectly reasonable. My husband will be glad to hear it." She smiled. "He was pretty worked up about it last night."

"Mine too," Mrs. Fullerton said. "I'll pass it on."

* * *

"A run?" Kenny gasped, when I broke the news in the locker room. "But—"

"This is *hockey*," Jeff interrupted. "Not gym class."

It was exactly what I'd been trying to tell Dad at the house. "But it's going to help us."

"Has your dad gone totally nuts?" Colin asked.

I didn't know what to say. Half the time, I was wondering the same thing and I wished we could just go back to the way Coach O'Neal ran practice. And the other half of the time I didn't want to go against my own dad in front of the guys. And of course a two-hour practice would be awesome.

"He's not nuts," I told them. "He knows what he's doing."

"It doesn't seem like it," Jeff said, through a hunk of beef jerky.

"Did you guys already forget that we won our last game?" I asked, trying to use Dad's logic.

"We would have won anyway," Jeff said.

"But maybe not by as many points," I reminded him.

"It *was* a record high," Patrick said.

Thank you!

"A win is a win," Jeff said. "We didn't beat those guys because we jumped up and down at the last practice."

Since Dad was showing no sign of going back to the way things were, I knew I had to get the guys to support him. "Look, my dad has bigger plans for us."

"What's that supposed to mean?" Colin asked.

"He's thinking long term, like winning the championship," I said. "You guys only care about the next game."

"Yeah, but if we don't think about the next game, we definitely won't need to think about the championship." Jeff snorted and his beef jerky fell on the floor. He picked it up and muttered "two-second rule" as he shoved it back into his mouth.

"He's got a bunch of ideas," I told the guys, hoping to convince them to give Dad a chance. "He's going to be moving us around and—"

"Moving us around what?" Colin asked, suspiciously.

"You know, changing positions and—"

"Changing positions?" Kenny practically screamed. "Why didn't you tell me?"

"Why didn't you tell any of us?" Colin asked.

Nuts!

"I'm not changing positions," Jeff said.

"Me neither," Colin agreed. "That's stupid."

"I wouldn't mind," Chris said, practically drooling at the idea of getting out of goal.

"Did you tell him it was a bad idea, Nugget?" Kenny asked.

"Yeah . . . I mean, I tried to, but . . . look, you're not listening to me," I said, getting frustrated. "The whole point is Dad wants us to have a great *season*, not just a great game."

"Then he should let us practice and play. The same way we have for our whole stinkin' lives," Jeff said.

"Yeah," Kenny sighed. "Changing positions? That's crazy."

I wanted to elbow him hard. He was supposed to back me up. "Come on, you guys," I said. "I know it's weird to be doing stuff differently, but—"

"It's two minutes to six," Bedhead said, finally waking up. "Practice is starting."

"No," Jeff said. "*Running* is starting."

"Huh?" Bedhead grunted.

I guess his branch of the phone tree had broken off. He was the only guy in uniform.

Colin double-knotted his shoelaces. "You know, it's pretty awesome that we all got up at five this morning to play hockey, and now we're going to be wasting our practice time pounding the pavement instead." He looked at the other guys before his eyes settled on me. "And somehow that's going to win us the championship?"

"Well, yeah," I said, shrugging. "I mean, it's training, right?"

"I could run at home," Colin snapped.

"Do you?" Bosko asked, from his spot in the corner.

"Do I what?"

"Run at home," Bosko said, giving him the stare-down.

It worked as well on Colin as it did on me, and all he could say was. "Well . . . no."

"So, what's your point?"

Colin's face turned red. "What's my . . . what's . . . what's *your* point, Bosko?"

"My point," Bosko said, in that deep voice, "is that when Coach says run—"

"We run?" Chris asked.

"Bingo," Bosko said.

Since everybody respected Bosko (a lot more than they respected me!), that ended the conversation and I didn't even hear any grumbling when they left in groups of two and three to meet Dad by the rink.

When it was down to just me and Bosko in the locker room, I felt like I had to say something. "Thanks for standing up for my dad. I mean, his practice ideas and all that."

Bosko shrugged. "I trust him. The guy almost went pro, so obviously he knows what he's doing."

"Yeah," I nodded.

"You should be backing him up, Nugget."

What?

"I have been," I told him. Wasn't he listening the whole time I tried to convince the guys?

"Not just in your head," he said, giving me that look. "Why should any of them trust what he says if his own kid doesn't?"

"Didn't you hear me? I was trying to tell them—"

"Not trying very hard," he said.

I sighed.

He was probably right.

Why did he always have to be right?

Geez, the guy was the same age as me, but he had to be a stinkin' genius about everything.

I wanted to be the guy who knew something for a change, so I said, "Well, I think it's cool that Dad's gonna mix the guys up a bit. You know, shuffle things around to try out some new combinations." Of course, he hadn't told me what those combinations were, but Bosko didn't know that.

"It's a good idea," Bosko said, nodding. "Fullerton would probably be better on defense, and I could see Colin covering goal."

"Really?" I was so used to everyone playing the same positions since we were five, it was hard to imagine any changes.

"I'm sure your dad has a plan," he said. "He knows what he's doing."

"I know," I told him, kind of ticked off. I was supposed to be the one telling *him* that Dad knew what he was doing.

Of course, I wasn't so sure about that, ten minutes into our run, when all I wanted to do was puke toast.

And twenty minutes later, when I actually did.

"Sorry, kiddo," Dad said, jogging in place next to me. "We'll just do cereal or something next time."

Great.

And things only got worse when we got back to the rink, all exhausted and sweaty.

We limped inside and headed straight for the ice to check out the other team's practice. All I saw was pink, pink and more pink. Even the puck was pink.

"No way," Kenny gasped. "Your dad gave our ice time to the Glitter?"

He was the only guy who could speak. The rest of the team just stared with their mouths hanging open.

"You've got to be kidding me," Colin finally muttered as a bunch of seven-year-old girls gobbled up our ice time.

* * *

I hate to say that the miserable "practice" ended up being the highlight of my day, but it was pretty close.

Sure, things went okay during gym class, when we played floor hockey, and the girls stopped yakking for long enough for Angela Fisker to make the best goal of the game. What a shot! She was so good, the Cougars could have used her.

And yes, it was nice when Mrs. Foster said my questions during English class showed "a surprisingly good understanding of the material."

But, as usual, Mr. Holloway's Math class brought the whole day screeching to a halt, like Wendy slamming on the minivan brakes.

I was in the middle of an awesome daydream about the Cougars winning the championship and Dad being voted Coach of the Year. I could practically see him lifting the trophy toward a cheering crowd and I guess I didn't hear Mr. Holloway over the imaginary fans.

But I heard the snickering around me.

"Mr. McDonald, please join us," Mr. Holloway said.

"I'm here," I said.

"In body, perhaps, but your mind seems to be travelling the globe. Please join me at the board," he said, waiting for me at the front of the classroom.

He'd probably said that six or seven thousand times since the school year started, and it was only November.

I was pretty sure I spent more time next to the board than the chalk did.

It wasn't fair.

Hadn't I already completed his Math hat trick last month?

Wasn't I already doing exactly what he needed me to do to pass the class?

He knew Bosko was tutoring me, he knew I worked almost as hard at Math as I did at hockey, and I guess he knew I wasn't an expert yet, because he called me to the board during almost every single class.

I tried not to psych myself out as I stood up.

Bosko gave me five on my way past his desk. "You can do it," he whispered.

I didn't even know what "it" was yet, but I nodded like I believed him.

I had to believe him.

I could do this!

When I got up to the board, Mr. Holloway handed me a piece of chalk, then started throwing out numbers, names, and a whole bunch of extra junk.

When he was done, my brain was still trying to catch up.

"Mr. McDonald?"

"Yes?"

"You appear somewhat stunned."

"No, I was . . . I just . . . wasn't that a word problem?"

A few of the kids giggled.

"Indeed it was, Mr. McDonald."

"But what about statistics?"

"Statistically speaking, I imagine you've listened to less than fifty percent of what I just told the class."

"Oh," I sighed.

"Today we are refreshing ourselves on what we have covered so far this year. We are doing this to ensure that we are prepared for the quiz this Friday."

"Quiz?" I asked.

"A small test," Mr. Holloway explained, like I didn't know what the word meant.

"I know it's—"

"Worth twenty percent of your grade."

I could barely swallow the lump in my throat. "Oh."

"Perhaps we should let someone else tackle the problem at hand and you can join me for a brief chat after class?"

Nuts.

It sounded like a question, but I was pretty sure it was a command. "Sure."

"I beg your pardon?"

Double nuts.

"Sorry, I meant to say yes."

I walked back to my seat and when I passed Bosko, he whispered, "What's wrong with you? We've done a thousand word problems."

"I don't know," I whispered back. "It caught me off guard."

I sat through the rest of class, worrying about what Mr. Holloway was going to say.

You'd think the guy would cut me some slack after I'd improved so much. He'd actually given me a high five after my last test, so how could I be back in the doghouse?

When the bell finally rang, I walked to his desk and took a deep breath. I had to be ready for anything.

"Mr. McDonald," he said, looking at me over his glasses. "I must admit I'm rather baffled and disappointed. I thought that your efforts outside of the classroom were proving beneficial."

"They are."

He frowned. "But you couldn't follow a simple word

problem today. Simpler than the tests you took last month, as a matter of fact."

"I guess I'm just out of practice," I told him, totally freaked out that he was going to make me do another set of tests. And if I failed, I didn't get to play hockey.

I waited, my palms getting all sweaty.

He was taking forever to drop the bomb on me.

"Perhaps this was a bad day for you," he finally said, quietly.

I looked up at him, surprised. "Maybe."

"Let's see how the quiz goes on Friday, shall we?"

I nodded, feeling totally relieved. "Okay . . . I mean, yes, please."

"If you disappoint me, we'll have to think about whether extracurricular activities are getting in the way of your academics again."

I didn't even have to ask what the big word was.

I knew he meant hockey.

Chapter Eleven

Just because Mr. Holloway was being weirdly nice about my problem at the chalkboard didn't mean Bosko would do the same. It was too bad my brain happened to freeze up on a tutoring day.

"Your place or the library?" he asked, when I met him in the hallway.

"My house. Wendy has volleyball practice."

We hadn't taken two steps before he was on me.

"Dude, what happened to you in there?"

I shrugged. "I don't know."

"I thought you were finished with being a flounder."

"I'm not a *flounder*," I muttered, as we walked toward the house.

"I don't know, Nugget. Thrashing around at the board with your mouth gaping open, like—"

Okay, already. "I was there, remember?"

"Look," Bosko said, "we went over word problems. You had a total handle on them."

"That's what I thought."

"You've got to focus. You can't just learn one thing and forget about it when we move onto the next thing."

"I know," I said, already sick of talking about it.

"It's all part of the same whole."

"Like fractions?" I asked, hoping to sound at least slightly smarter than usual.

"No, it's . . . like a hockey team, man."

I rolled my eyes. "Yeah, right."

"I'm serious. You've got to have all the parts. A goalie, defensemen, centre and wingers."

I stared at him. "We only play one position at a time."

He frowned. "That's actually a good point. Okay, I take it back. Math isn't like a hockey team, but you get what I'm saying, right?"

"I guess. We need all the parts and I can't forget old stuff when I learn new stuff," I told him.

He nodded. "So, what did Holloway say?"

"He's going to see how I do on the quiz."

"That's it?" he asked, looking as surprised as I was.

"Yup."

"Nice. We'll just have to make sure you ace it."

"Get serious, Bosko."

"Okay, 'ace' might be pushing it, but you made B's on his tests before. You can do it again."

We walked in silence for a block or so.

Bosko wasn't the kind of guy who talked for the sake of talking, which was kind of cool. Except for the fact that when he wasn't talking I was pretty sure he was thinking about what an idiot I was.

"What are you thinking?" I asked, when I couldn't take it any more.

He snorted. "You sound like my mum."

"Oh."

"I'm not thinking about anything."

"Cool," I said, shoving my hands in my pockets. "You don't have to tell me."

"No, I don't," he said, then glanced at me and sighed. "You really want to know?"

"Yeah."

"Okay, I'm thinking about logarithms."

"Log-a what?"

"It's Math. Like, advanced Math." He laughed. "You want to hear more?"

"No way," I sighed.

When we got to the house, Mum had made her special oatmeal raisin cookies, which happened to be one of Bosko's favourites.

"I could eat these all day," he said, grabbing a handful, like I wouldn't want any.

Like they weren't for both of us.

I grabbed three for myself. I had the lead in goals, and I'd have a cookie lead too.

"I'm glad you like them," Mum said. "Do you think your mother might want the recipe?"

"She doesn't use recipes."

"Oh, I wish I had a memory like that," Mum said, smiling.

"No, I mean she only bakes things that come in a tube."

"A tube?" Mum asked, frowning.

"You know, kind of already made, like you just put the dough on the tray and heat it up."

Mum looked like her world was crumbling faster than a store-bought cupcake. "I see," she said, quietly. "I'll send you home with a little bag of these."

What?

I *loved* her oatmeal raisin! They should have gone in my lunch.

"Seriously?" Bosko asked.

"Yes," Mum laughed.

I grabbed another one.

Nugget: ahead by one goal and three cookies.

When she left us alone, we got right down to business, but I managed to snag a couple more cookies while Bosko was digging in his backpack.

As we got started, I was surprised that when he reminded me about some of the stuff I'd already learned and had me practise some examples, it came back to me.

"See?" he said. "It's in there. You just have to dig it out."

I sure hoped he was right.

If I didn't pass the test and Mr. Holloway hit the brakes on my hockey season, Dad would be on his own.

And without me there to support him, would the guys even give him a chance?

I didn't want to find out.

* * *

We actually got out on the ice for our two-hour practice on Wednesday. I was excited to be back on track until Dad was in the middle of explaining a new drill and our benchwarmers, Curtis Blank and Tim Shaw, skated away from the group with a puck and started playing a quiet game of keep-away.

"Guys, I'm going to need you to join the rest of us," Dad said.

"We're okay over here, Mr. McDonald," Curtis called over his shoulder.

What?

"Practice is happening over here, guys," Dad said, sounding annoyed.

They acted like they hadn't heard him.

I was too stunned to do anything. I'd never ignored an adult when they told me to do something. Especially a coach. And sub or not, Dad *was* the coach.

Before I knew what was happening, Colin skated over and started to play too. Then Jeff.

"Geez," Patrick whispered. "Bad idea."

I just nodded.

What was Dad supposed to do? Yell at them? Threaten them with a time-out?

He looked as unsure as I was, then cleared his throat.

"If you do not get over here—" Dad started, but before he could get the rest of his sentence out, Bosko had taken off like a freakin' bullet train.

In a matter of seconds, he had Tim and Curtis by their jerseys and was dragging them back to the rest of the team.

When he shoved them down on the ice at centre, he looked back at Jeff and Colin. "Am I going to have to come get you, too?"

They only looked at each other for a split second before they both hustled back to the rest of us.

Bosko took his time giving each of the guys the kind of steely look I could never pull off.

"Respect the coach, you jerks," he growled.

Dad cleared his throat. "Okay, so back to the drill."

I didn't listen to the rest of it. Instead, I stood there, wishing I'd been the one to put a stop to the situation. But of course it was Bosko.

After the first hour, which was jam-packed with drills, Dad finally let us *play*.

But there was a catch.

"Okay, I'm going to try something new here," he said,

checking his notepad while we sat in a circle on the ice. "Bosko, let's give you a shot at centre."

"Centre?" Bosko asked, surprised.

"Yes," Dad nodded, "as in middle."

"Okay," he said, with a shrug.

I'd been thinking about this change from the second Dad mentioned it. At first I'd been excited because Bosko would be out of his element, but the more I thought about it, the more I realized that he was actually going to be in prime shooting position.

Gretzky played centre, for crying out loud.

That meant Bosko would be scoring more than anyone. The rest of us would be feeding him the puck from every angle.

And how was I supposed to score more goals?

Was Dad going to move me to centre too?

He had to!

"Now, Colin, I want to put you in as right defense."

"But I'm left wing," Colin told him. "I've been left wing since I was like, born."

"Which is exactly why changing things up a bit is a good idea," Dad explained. "You guys are too locked into your roles."

"That's because we're good at them," Colin said.

"Hey," Dad said, "we don't know what we're capable of until we try. Look at Wendel Clark."

"Who?" Kenny asked.

"A totally famous Leaf," I told him. I'd just read his stats in *Shoot! Volume 4*.

"I've never heard of him," Kenny said.

"Only because he didn't play for Detroit," I told him.

"Back in '85," Dad explained, "he was drafted by the

Maple Leafs as a defenseman, but ended up being one of the best forwards the Leafs ever had."

"Yeah, well what about Wade Belak?" Colin demanded. "Same team, same plan, total disaster."

Wade Belak? What had Colin been reading? I'd have to find Belak in the "Shoot" series.

Dad frowned. "I'm not saying the plan is foolproof."

"That's for sure," Colin muttered.

"Just let him coach, Bechter," Bosko said, and that, as usual, was enough to shut Colin up.

"Kenny," Dad continued, "I'm going to move you to left wing. I watched you do a great job on the line a few weeks ago."

"Awesome!" Kenny grinned.

"Oh, brother," Colin sighed, as he slumped on the bench and rested his head in his hands.

"Patrick?" Dad asked.

"Yes?" he answered, looking excited.

"I'm going to keep you where you are, as left defense."

"Oh," Patrick said, looking disappointed.

I kept waiting for Dad to assign me a position, but the only ones left were my usual spot at right wing or goalie.

Was he going to dump me on the bench?

"McCafferty?"

Bedhead didn't speak up, and when I turned to look at him, he was asleep, his head resting on his knees.

I nudged his skate with mine, and he jolted awake.

"McCafferty?" Dad asked again.

"Here," Bedhead said, like it was a roll call at school.

"I'm putting you in goal."

Oh no!

"What?" he asked, rubbing his eyes. "Why?"

"He's mixing things up," Colin explained, lifting his head and looking steamed. "We're going to be all mixed up."

"I said 'changing things up,' Colin," Dad told him firmly.

"Whatever," Colin sighed.

"Goalie?" Bedhead said, scratching his chin. "That seems kind of nuts."

"No," Kenny said, barely loud enough for me to hear him. "It seems *totally* nuts."

"Nugget," Dad said, "You stay at right wing."

My mouth dried up. If Bosko was at centre and I was only playing right wing, he would totally win our scoring contest!

"Why does he get to keep his position?" Colin asked.

"Because that's what I'm telling him to do," Dad said.

"But everyone else had to switch," Kenny said, frowning.

"Not me," Patrick muttered.

"Guys, enough chatter, already," Dad said.

Everyone took off to warm up, whispering and snorting about what a joke it all was. Dad stayed with Chris and Bedhead to help switch the goalie gear from one to the other.

Chris looked totally happy to give it up.

Bedhead looked . . . awake, for a change.

I tried to look at the bright side. I'd still be playing a position I knew and was awesome at, which meant I'd be in the zone while the rest of the guys were still figuring out their new slots.

The scrimmage went pretty well, even though we had some sloppy moments. By the end, everyone seemed okay with having tried something new.

That is, until Dad told us we'd be trying them out again at the next game.

"What?" Colin choked. "I've been a defenseman for less than an hour."

"I'm talking about trying it out, not doing it full-time," Dad told him. "We're not changing positions for the whole game, but I'm going to give each of you some minutes in your backup positions."

"That's crazy," Colin said.

"What's crazy," Dad corrected, "is having one goalie and no one to fill in when he moved away. What's *crazy* is waiting for that to happen to your best centre or defenseman and having no backup plan."

I had to admit, he had a point there. Rotating guys through goal had been a mess. And if we lost a player again, who knew what could go wrong.

"Now, I'd like to talk to you guys about a team captain," Dad said, at the end of practice.

We'd never replaced Jason when he moved away, so it was about time.

"How do we pick?" Colin asked.

"A simple vote," Dad said, pulling stubby pencils and slips of paper from his inside coat pocket. "Everybody fill in the name of the guy you'd like to act as leader and represent you to the officials. And don't vote for yourselves, please."

This was going to be awesome!

I'd always dreamed of being team captain. And I couldn't imagine the guys picking anyone else. I was one of the most dedicated players, with the highest number of goals on the team. I got along with everybody and come on, my dad was the coach.

Or would that count against me?

If the guys didn't like the way Dad was running practices, would they take it out on me?

I scribbled Kenny's name on my scrap of paper, knowing I'd be the only one to vote for him. No risk there.

I watched as the other guys turned in their scraps and waited while Dad tallied them up.

"One for Fullerton," he said. "One for Bosko."

What? Who voted for Bosko?

"Two for Bosko," Dad continued. "One for Chen. One for McDonald."

Finally!

"Two for McDonald. Oh, three for McDonald."

Yes!

"Three for Bosko. Four for Bosko."

But I was the only guy on the team who liked Bosko! And even though this wasn't a popularity contest . . . it kind of was.

"Two for Fullerton. Five for Bosko."

Had they all forgotten the power play he caused in the Thunder game? We lost the game because of Bosko's temper!

"Seven for Bosko," Dad said. "Congratulations to our new team captain, Eddie Bosko."

I couldn't believe it.

* * *

When we all hit the locker room, the guys didn't waste any time.

"Nugget, you need to talk to your dad," Jeff said.

I pretended I didn't know what he was talking about. "I talk to him every day."

Jeff scowled. "You know what I mean."

"About the drills and position changes and stuff?" I asked.

"Yes," Curtis, Jeff and Colin all hissed at the same time.

"This plyo-whatever junk is a joke," Fullerton said.

"Yeah," Colin added, "And these new positions? Your dad's clueless."

I took a run at him, but Patrick and Kenny held me back. "Don't talk about him like that," I growled.

"I can say what I want," Colin told me. "My dad says he's already screwing up our season."

"Well, you and your dad can just wait till Saturday's game. You'll be eating those words."

"Whatever, Nugget," he said, rolling his eyes.

The guys let go of me and I was disappointed to see that most of the team seemed to be siding with Colin. They didn't even make eye contact with me.

"I'm serious," I told the whole locker room. "Saturday's game will be a massacre."

No one said anything, but at least Patrick Chen gave me a high five when he and a couple of other guys left.

Pretty soon it was just Bosko and me in the locker room. Again.

"I can't believe the guys don't get what Dad's trying to do," I said.

"I can," Bosko said, with a smirk.

"What do you mean?"

Bosko shook his head. "They're different from you and me, Nugget."

I stopped what I was doing. Him and me? Bosko thought we were the same? "Really?"

He leaned on his stick. "All these guys care about is scrimmages and Saturday games."

"Don't you?"

"Of course," he said, laughing. "But I care about the championship too. And next season, and the season after that."

"So do I," I said, shrugging.

"Exactly. And we care about getting into Junior, right?"

"Well, yeah, because if we don't play Junior—"

"We never make it to the NHL," he finished.

I smiled. Bosko had the same dream I did. "Right."

"I don't want to just play hockey when I'm a kid and then grow out of it."

"Me neither."

"I want it to be my life. My career."

"Me too," I told him. "I want to be Jean Ducette."

"Oh yeah?" He laughed again. "Well, I want to be Eddie Bosko."

"Well, yeah. I mean, I want to be me, but—"

"Eddie Bosko, starting right winger for the Chicago Blackhawks." He smiled enough to show some of the teeth I used to think were fangs.

"Nugget McDonald, starting right winger for the Vancouver Canucks," I said, smiling too.

"That's what I'm talking about. We're the same."

"The same," I said, nodding.

"And that means we both know that we have a lot of work to do," Bosko said, shrugging. "I'm not going to whine about training if it means I end up a pro. Get me?"

"Yeah," I nodded, suddenly understanding why the guys had voted him team captain.

"We're the ones who want it most," he said.

And he was right.

I knew in my heart that I was more dedicated to hockey than most of the guys on the team.

I wanted it more.

And so did Bosko.

So, how could we convince the rest of the Cougars to play along?

Chapter Twelve

I was still thinking about Friday's Math quiz when I woke up on Saturday morning. As usual, I had no idea how I'd done, and Mr. Holloway was going to mark the stupid thing over the weekend.

As if he needed two whole days!

Even though I knew he had to mark everybody's quizzes and he wasn't trying to punish me, I wished he'd just whipped through it on Friday afternoon and saved me the torture.

I thought about it all the way to Esquimalt, and that was a long ride.

Three of the other team mums had gotten up early that morning to drive us to the game in a minivan caravan. Mum drove the fourth van, with me, Dad, Kenny and Bedhead McCafferty as passengers. The other guys slept most of the way there while us McDonalds talked.

Dad was ready to play us in our new positions, and I was worried.

An hour of practising a totally new position didn't seem

like nearly enough. It was like teaching a kid how to doggie paddle and tossing him in the Pacific.

And new positions during a *game*?

"Today is the perfect time to try them out," Dad had told me. "You're playing a much weaker team. It's almost like a practice instead of a game, anyway."

I leaned back in my seat and sighed.

Thinking about it kind of made my stomach hurt.

Especially when I pictured Bosko at centre and all the goals he could score.

He would beat me in the competition, he'd already beaten me for team captain. What if he ended up being the season's MVP?

I was starting to get a headache.

For once, I didn't want to think about hockey, so I daydreamed about the growth spurt Mum kept promising instead. I stared out the window, wondering when I'd at least break the tie between me and Ella Patterson for shortest kid in grade six.

Mum and Dad started going over their plans for new carpet in the living room and pretty soon I was asleep too.

I mean, who could talk about carpets for longer than forty-five seconds?

When I woke up, we were pulling into the Esquimalt rink.

"Ready?" Dad asked, as me and the guys stretched and yawned.

I didn't have to think too hard about that. Dad was right about Esquimalt being weaker than us. They were the lowest ranking team in the league, which meant we were practically guaranteed a win.

And the guys couldn't complain if we were in the middle of a winning streak, right?

"Definitely ready," I said, jumping out of the car.

Judging by the chatter in the locker room, which was mostly about how we were going to wipe the ice with the Eagles, it seemed like all of us were ready.

But it turned out that we weren't even close.

* * *

The funny thing about the Eagles was that they weren't only the worst team in the league, but the weirdest looking. Most of the guys in our age group were about the same size (except for me being a shrimp and a guy like Bosko looking like a gorilla), but the Eagles were all over the place.

They had a goalie who was built like a toothpick and constantly had pucks whizzing by his skinny arms. Then they had a great big centre who couldn't skate if his life depended on it, and a couple of slouching wingers who always looked more interested in watching the game than playing in it.

When you added their green and brown uniforms, the whole thing just looked ugly.

Just before game time, Dad told us we'd be starting off in our new positions. I took a deep breath, waiting for the guys to try to change his mind, but they kept pretty quiet. Maybe they'd decided it wasn't such a bad idea.

At least that's what I thought until I heard Jeff talking to Colin about Dad picking favourites by keeping me at right wing. I didn't like the sound of that at all.

He wasn't playing favourites. After all, Bosko was the one who'd end up being a scoring machine.

I had to keep up with him, so I knew I had to play one of the most awesome games of my life.

Again.

So I did, from the second the puck was dropped.

But the rest of the guys? They stunk like week-old garbage.

Bedhead was so bad as a goalie, we would have been better off with an empty net.

Seriously.

Kenny wasn't aggressive enough with the Eagles' offense, and they kept blowing past him like he was a ghost.

A whiny ghost.

And the biggest surprise was Bosko.

As worried as I was about him being in prime goal-scoring position, I'd found a silver lining. I'd thought about great NHL partners, like Robitaille and Gretzky or Detroit's Production Line, who I read about in *Shoot! Volume 1*.

Bosko at centre could actually be a good thing.

I'd convinced myself that we could become an awesome duo too, so I was half relieved and half disappointed when he couldn't get it together at all. It was like he was playing for the first time.

"What's your deal?" I asked, near the end of the first period, when we were both back on the bench to catch our breath.

"My deal? I've never played centre in my entire life."

"I can tell."

"What did you say?" he growled.

"I said—"

"Say it again and I'll pop you one, Nugget."

"Okay, okay. Look, it's just like playing right but, you know . . . in the middle."

"Thanks for the update, genius."

"I'm just saying—"

"If you think you could handle it, trade me."

"Trade you what?"

"Let me play right wing and you mess around in the middle."

"I can't just switch," I told him. "Dad . . . I mean, Coach put me here."

"How convenient," Jeff said. "You're the only guy playing your normal position."

"*And* I've scored three goals," I reminded them.

I was four ahead of Bosko for the season!

He hadn't scored once.

"My point, exactly," Bosko grunted.

The guys never got their momentum going in the new positions, and the fans who'd travelled to the game started to get pretty loud about it.

"You need to put Colin back at left wing!" Mrs. Bechter yelled. "That other kid doesn't know which end is up!"

"And move Chris back into goal," Fullerton's mum shouted. "He's way better than the guy you've got in there."

"No, Mum," Chris begged from the bench, happy to be out of the net.

"This should be a slaughter," his mother said.

"We're winning," I muttered. Barely, but winning.

"Bosko hasn't had a single goal," Kenny said. "That's a pretty good sign that something's gone haywire."

"Your dad isn't going to switch everybody back to their normal positions, is he?" Chris asked, looking worried.

"He'd better," Kenny said.

"I think so," I told them. "But I don't know when."

"Maybe once you've scored double digits?" Bosko asked.

"Very funny," I said.

"No," Bosko growled. "Not funny at all."

Colin's mum showed up behind the bench to talk to Dad.

"Why is your kid still in position?" she asked.

"Because that's where I put him," Dad told her.

"But—"

"I'm not going to argue with you," Dad told her, crossing his arms and turning back toward the game.

Even though I was playing awesome, I started wishing Dad would move me somewhere else, so I could be as crummy as everyone else.

The guys thought I was getting special treatment, and I hated it.

So why didn't Dad just switch me?

In the second period I was back in the game, which was great. Except for the fact that the better I played, the worse I felt.

Dad finally moved everyone back to their old positions late in the period, but it was too late.

Even back where they belonged, the guys couldn't get it together. They were so frustrated by how things had gone in their new slots, they couldn't get their heads in the game.

When there was only a minute and a half left on the clock and the game was tied up, Bosko kind of lost it.

One of the Eagles blocked his shot and Bosko charged him.

"It's déjà vu all over again," Dad said, as our gorilla was sent to the box.

Geez, if Dad's strategies didn't sink the team, Bosko's temper would.

We only had four guys left on the ice and the Eagles scored again.

It was the shock of the century when we lost the game, 5–4.

Just before we left for the locker room, Colin told my

dad, "Didn't someone tell you once that it's about hockey, not humiliation?"

Dad didn't say a word.

* * *

When we got home, after a long, mostly silent drive, the answering machine was flashing eleven messages.

Five of them were from Colin's dad, wondering why his kid wasn't playing the right position.

Two were from Kenny's dad, asking what on earth Dad had been thinking and threatening to call Coach O'Neal.

Three were Kenny's mum, trying to talk louder than his dad, who was still yelling in the background.

The final message was from Coach O'Neal, asking Dad to call him back.

"I waited too long," Dad said, with a deep sigh. "I should have switched everybody back sooner."

Obviously!

"Why didn't you?" I asked.

"Because they'd done so well at practice. I just kept waiting for things to click into place."

"But when the worst team in the league was catching up to us . . ."

"I know, Nugget," he said, shaking his head. "But my plan really should have worked."

Dad went upstairs to call Coach from the phone in the office and I was glad I didn't have to overhear it.

* * *

"So?" Mum asked when he came back downstairs, twenty minutes later.

"He'd heard from some parents," Dad told her.

Uh-oh.

"And?" Mum asked.

"He thinks the position changes are a good idea, considering the hole that was left in goal when Jason moved."

"That's good," Mum said, nodding.

"He'd heard about the ice time too, so I explained that we get make-up time at the Wednesday practices. He was fine with that."

Mum smiled. "This all sounds very positive."

"It was, until we talked about today's loss."

"Oh." She frowned.

"Let's just say Coach O'Neal was *disappointed* that we lost to such a low-ranking team."

I'm glad I didn't hear the actual words he used.

"What's the verdict?" Mum asked.

"He told me to tone down the changes. He said it's too much at once."

Great. That meant even Coach was mad at Dad.

"If that's what Coach wants, you should probably—" Mom began.

"Don't worry, hon," Dad interrupted, giving her a squeeze. "I know what I'm doing and I'm going to show everybody."

Those were not the words I wanted to hear.

Everything was so messed up, I wasn't even hungry for dinner. I barely ate any of my chicken, and my corn on the cob, which I usually wolfed down, just sat there on the plate.

When Dad invited me to watch the Leafs game with him later that night, I just shook my head and started toward the stairs.

"It's a game, son." Dad called after me. "Sometimes you lose."

Yeah, right.

But not to the freakin' Eagles.

Chapter Thirteen

Mondays were always rotten, but knowing I had practice right off the bat made it a thousand times worse.

I hated the fact that the parents had ganged up on Dad and ratted him out to Coach. And I hated the fact that Dad didn't seem to be giving up on his master plans.

We didn't talk much during breakfast and I could tell he was thinking about all kinds of stuff.

I was doing the same thing.

What stunk the most about how things were turning out was that I'd been so excited about Dad coaching the team. I was tired of the guys giving him a hard time and even more tired of Dad doing his own thing.

And losing to the Eagles?

That was the worst of it.

I had to do something.

"Dad, can you please just go back to practising like Coach did?"

He took a bite of toast. "There's nothing wrong with what we're doing."

"Except it's not working," I said, getting frustrated.

Why couldn't he see that?

"I disagree, Nugget. And even if it *wasn't* working right away, we'd still need to give new ideas time to see how they developed."

I took a deep breath. "What's developing is really mad parents."

Dad stopped chewing and stared at me. "I know what I'm doing, son, and I'm not about to start taking orders from a bunch of spectators who don't have a clue."

"But when Coach O'Neal—"

"I appreciate Coach's advice, but—"

"It wasn't advice, Dad. He was telling you what he wants you to do."

Dad sighed. "Look, Nugget. Coach is from a different era in sports, an older generation. They did things differently back then. Soon enough, he'll see that what I'm doing is helping the team and he'll appreciate it. Plyometrics and position changes could be the ticket to the championship."

I couldn't think of anything else to say and he obviously wasn't going to listen, anyway.

Fine.

I'd tried really hard to support him, but was I supposed to sit back and let him destroy the team?

* * *

When I got to the locker room that morning, it was pretty obvious that most of the guys were siding with the angry parents.

Kenny even caught a ride to practice with Colin instead of us that morning. While we got changed, he was looking anywhere but at me.

Other than Bosko, who hadn't shown up yet, only a couple of guys were siding with Dad, and they were the ones who didn't say much, like Patrick Chen and the Watson triplets. Geez, I wasn't even on Dad's side anymore.

"Let me guess," Colin said, with a smirk. "Plyometrics today, Nugget?"

I shook my head. "We're running."

"So, the Glitter will be using our ice time again?" Kenny groaned.

"You know we'll get a two-hour practice on Wednesday, just like last time," I reminded him.

"For practising the wrong positions," Colin said.

I was pretty sure running was the worst decision Dad could have made. Up until the nasty phone calls, he'd been planning to spend Monday's practice on the ice. He'd even told me there would definitely be a scrimmage because he wanted the guys to get more comfortable in their new positions.

But that plan was out the window (and run over by a Mack truck) because midway through the Leafs game, he got the phone tree started, letting everyone know it was an off-ice practice.

I wished he could see that giving in to what everybody wanted wasn't the end of the world. Geez, he and Mum were always talking about compromise.

Losing to the Eagles was the lowest and most depressing point in my whole hockey career and we needed to get back to the way things were.

Did he have to be so stubborn?

Was it really that big a deal to let us play hockey at hockey practice?

"I think this is stupid," Colin said, as he laced up his running shoes. "This isn't even hockey anymore."

"Totally," Kenny nodded.

The guys looked pretty surprised when I nodded too.

"What's going on, Nugget?" Chris asked.

"Nothing," I said, shrugging. I was tired of all the drama.

"Is there something you aren't telling us?" Colin asked, "*Again?*"

"No, I'm just . . . I'm frustrated too."

"So do something about it," Colin said. "He's your dad."

"Look, I've tried talking to him and he won't listen."

"Maybe we should go on strike," Jeff suggested.

"Yeah," a couple of the guys agreed.

What?

"Brilliant idea," Patrick said, sarcastically. "Then we don't have a season at all."

"Better than a losing season," Colin muttered.

"No it isn't," Patrick told the whole group as he dropped his bag on the bench. "Any season is better than none. Don't you guys remember when we were little and the whole NHL went on strike?"

"No," Colin snapped.

"I do," Kenny sighed. "It stunk."

"I know," I said, remembering a fact I'd read. "It was the only year since 1919 that no one got a Stanley Cup. They didn't play a single game."

No one said anything.

"Look, a little running isn't going to kill us," Patrick said. "And we'll be back on the ice for double the time at our next practice."

"Things better start turning around here," Colin said, pushing past me and heading for the rink, Kenny right on his tail. "Or else."

"Or else what?" Patrick asked, but didn't get an answer.

"Are you coming, Nugget?" Colin called over his shoulder as he led Kenny and Jeff out to the hallway.

I looked at Patrick, who'd stood up for Dad, and I felt my face turn red.

"Bosko would have said something," Patrick said quietly. "Bosko would have shut them up."

"Yeah, but he's not here," I said quietly.

Where the heck was he? Dad's best supporter was gone.

In that second, I decided to follow the guys and leave Patrick, Bedhead and Dad's other supporters behind. I was glad Bosko wasn't there to see it.

I walked down the hallway, surprised that he was a no-show. He never missed practice.

Ever.

When I got to the rink, the guys were all standing around, totally quiet.

Dad was nowhere in sight.

"What's going on?" I asked.

"My dad and Mr. Cavanaugh are here to talk to your dad," Colin said, with a smirk.

I could hear voices near the concession stand, so I walked over, feeling my palms getting sweaty. I heard the rest of the guys following behind me, whispering.

When I got to the three dads, they were all red-faced.

Uh-oh.

"You're not even qualified to coach," Mr. Bechter said.

What?

I felt like I'd been slapped in the face, and Dad looked like he actually had been.

Then Kenny's dad said, "Yeah, *almost* being a Flame isn't the same as actually being one, Gord."

"I never said it was," Dad told them. He looked seriously

steamed. "And I have nothing to prove to either of you. If you felt this strongly about it, you should have volunteered to cover for Coach O'Neal."

"I wasn't—" Mr. Bechter started, but Dad cut him off.

"Here?" Dad asked. "Of course you weren't. You haven't been to a single game this season."

"But—"

"You just introduced yourself to me because I've never even seen you in the seven years these boys have been playing together."

Mr. Bechter's face turned an even deeper shade of red.

"Yeah, well I've been here and—" Mr. Cavanaugh started.

"And you have full knowledge of the sport?" Dad asked, looking doubtful.

"Yes!" Kenny's dad said, and some blobs of spit shot into the air.

Gross.

"Okay, I'm going to test you on that, Glen. If one of our players cross-checks the other team's goalie while he's in the crease, what happens?"

"A major penalty," Kenny's dad said, shaking his head like it was a dumb question.

"And?" Dad asked.

"And what?"

"I'm asking you, Glen."

"He's off to the penalty box." Kenny's dad shook his head again, but this time he didn't look as sure.

"The ref's also going to call a Game Misconduct."

Kenny's dad frowned. "So?"

"So you need to know the rules to coach, Glen. How about another one?" Dad asked, then didn't wait for an answer. "Let's say Kenny breaks his stick out there."

"He drops the broken pieces on the ice, then gets rid of them," Mr. Cavanaugh said, like he was some kind of genius.

"And then he does what?" Dad asked.

"This is ridiculous," Mr. Bechter said, shaking his head.

"*He gets a new one,*" Mr. Cavanaugh said, rolling his eyes.

"What if the broken stick belongs to the goalie?"

"Same thing," Mr. Cavanaugh said, shrugging.

"So, the goalie picks up a new one from the team bench?"

"Obviously."

"Only if he wants a Delay of Game penalty," Dad said.

"What?"

Dad shook his head. "You can say what you want about my methods, but the simple fact is that I'm the only guy who stepped in for Coach O'Neal. Now, until you've read the Rule Book from start to finish, don't waste any more of our practise time."

The two dads looked at each other, then at all of us.

"Colin, get over here," Mr. Bechter said. "We're leaving."

Colin looked shocked. "But Dad—"

"*Now.*"

For a kid who'd been ready to go on strike, Colin looked miserable as he walked back to the locker room.

"You too, Kenny," Mr. Cavanaugh said. "Get your gear and let's get out of here." When Kenny walked away with his head hanging down, Mr. Cavanaugh turned to Dad. "This isn't the end of the discussion," he said as he and Mr. Bechter turned toward the exit.

"Not by a long shot," Mr. Bechter added.

And then they were gone.

Jeff looked at me. "Are you gonna stay?"

"Well . . . yeah. What about you?"

"I don't want to leave," he said, shrugging.

I waited for Dad to say what jerks those dads were, but he didn't. He blew his whistle instead.

"The clock is ticking, guys," he said. "Let's hit the pavement."

As we jogged through the dark streets in sprinkling rain, the guys were pretty quiet. The only comments I heard were about how cool Patrick thought it was when Dad stood up to the other men, and how stupid they looked when he started quizzing them. "Mr. McDonald really knows his stuff," Patrick said.

"Well, duh," Jeff said, like he hadn't been siding with Colin all along. "The guy was a ref, for crying out loud. He's an expert."

I kept pace with the rest of the guys, but on my own and off to the side, so I could think.

I was super proud of the way Dad had stood up to those guys, and they'd definitely ended up looking foolish. But while Patrick had taken over sticking up for him, I'd been stupid enough to follow Colin.

Now Jeff had switched sides and I felt like an idiot.

Nothing was going the way it should.

And the biggest problem of all?

The Cougars might have to win without Colin and Kenny.

And how were we supposed to do that?

* * *

I didn't expect to see Bosko at school, since he wasn't at practice, but once Math class rolled around, there he was, looking like nothing had happened.

"Where were you this morning?" I asked.

"In bed," he said, digging into his pack.

"In bed," I repeated.

"Yeah, I slept in."

"And missed practice," I said, even though he already knew that.

Bosko stared at me. "You got it."

"Well, are you going to be there on Wednesday?"

"Probably."

"Bosko," I sighed. "I don't know if you heard what happened this morning, but—"

"Yup."

"Okay, so we've got no Kenny or Colin now. And you know if you miss the practice right before the game, you don't play."

"I know, Nugget." He dropped his books on his desk with a thud. "Look, I had to talk my dad out of coming down this morning, okay?"

"Seriously?" I'd never seen Bosko's dad before, but imagined he had a lot in common with King Kong.

"Yeah. He's not too crazy about the whole centre thing."

"But—"

"And neither am I."

"Obviously. Nice penalty to finish off the game."

He glared at me. "I've been the best player on every team I've been on for my entire life."

Was he including the Cougars? Because I was pretty sure I was outscoring him.

"Do you know what it was like not to score a single goal on Saturday?"

"Um . . ."

"Of course you don't," he snorted. "You were too busy being the star."

"Okay, okay," I said. "But did you have to charge that kid?"

"I was mad, Nugget. So yeah, I did."

"Even though it cost the team?" I challenged.

"Right now *everything* is costing the team. I like your dad and I get what he's trying to do, but there's no way I'm gonna play like that again."

"Bosko, centre doesn't have to be a bad thing."

"Why, because you'll outscore me for the season?"

"No, it could be a really good thing. Just think . . . we could be like the Sedin twins—"

He laughed. "Yeah, right. I'm about three feet taller than you."

It was a total exaggeration (he was maybe two feet taller), but I let it go.

"I don't mean the twin part, but the awesome duo part."

"Whatever," he said, shaking his head.

"I think Dad's on to something," I told him, taking the opportunity to stick up for Dad after I'd blown it that morning. "Look at Jamie Benn."

"From Dallas? I hate the Stars."

"My point is that they switched him from wing to centre and he's playing awesome."

"Nugget," Bosko sighed.

"Did you know Mark Messier played left wing before he switched to centre?"

"Yup."

I wasn't expecting that, so I had to think fast. "The guy won six Stanley Cups, Bosko."

"Last time I checked, we were a kids' team in an island league. I don't think we're in the running for a Stanley Cup this season."

"You're the one who was talking about an NHL career and working hard. Why can't you see the big picture here?"

He gave me the stare-down. "Why don't you draw it for me?"

"Paired up on the ice, we can be even stronger than ever."

"It's not about that," he sighed. "It's about right wing. *Gordie Howe* played right wing."

"He was ambidextrous." I had to look the word up when I read it in *Shoot! Volume 2*, so I knew it meant he was both left- and right-handed.

"Yeah, but he *always* played right wing. Him, Brett Hull, The Rocket. They all played right wing."

"Yeah, but centre? Geez, man. Gretzky, Lemieux, Yzerman," I counted off, glad I had plenty of ammo. "Federov played centre *and* right wing *and* defense. Bosko, you're the freakin' Sergei Federov of Vancouver Island if you pull this off."

"Exactly, Nugget. *If.* And you saw what happened at Saturday's game."

"I know. But you have to at least try."

Bosko was quiet and I couldn't tell if I'd managed to change his mind.

"Look," he finally said. "I respect your dad, and I respect his coaching, okay? I don't like the idea of centre, but I'll roll with the position change if I have to."

Yes!

"Cool," I said, nodding.

"Yeah, well, my dad won't be quite as cool. It was better to miss practice this morning than let him chew your dad up."

Chew him up?

I swallowed hard. "Thanks, man."

"No problem," he said. "For now, anyway."

I sat at my desk and waited for Mr. Holloway to pass all of the tests back.

I closed my eyes and imagined a seventy-five or an eighty marked in red ink at the top of the page. All of Bosko's tutoring had to pay off, didn't it?

I opened my eyes when I heard the teacher's steps walking toward me.

"Mr. McDonald," he said, handing me the page and giving me a slight nod.

Barely breathing, I glanced at the page.

A seventy-seven.

Yes!

Bosko turned to face me and I whispered my score.

He gave me a thumbs-up.

Whew.

So, Math wasn't going to keep me off the ice (for that week, anyway). I closed my eyes again, totally relieved.

After all, without Kenny and Colin, the Cougars' hockey season was in more than enough trouble already.

Chapter Fourteen

Bosko and I left Mr. Holloway's class together, ready to head to the library for tutoring. But I hadn't even made it to my locker when I heard my name over the P.A. system.

"Jonathan McDonald, please report to the principal's office."

What?

"Busted," Bosko, said, punching my shoulder.

"I didn't do anything," I told him.

"That's your story. Stick to it," he laughed.

I couldn't think of a single thing I'd done that would get me sent to the office. Geez, I'd been in school all stinkin' day!

As Bosko and I walked, a bunch of kids made stupid comments about what kind of trouble I was in.

When we finally got there, I walked in the door and almost crashed into my sister.

"What are you doing here?" I asked.

"Picking you up, dork." She pulled her purse onto her shoulder and walked past me and Bosko, who was staring at her, as usual.

My sister was almost six feet tall and ninety percent of her height was legs. She walked in huge steps and I was always hurrying to catch up.

But not Bosko. My giant was right at her side, grinning like a fool.

"Where are we going?" I called out to her.

"Where do you think?" she asked, over her shoulder.

"I don't know. The mall?"

"Ha! As if I'd be seen with you toads at the mall."

Hadn't she tried dragging me there just a few days ago?

"Then where?"

"Home, dummy."

"But we're going to the library," I told her.

"Not anymore."

"Wendy, seriously, what's going on?"

She stopped and turned to face me with her hands on her hips. "The only way Mum would let me borrow the van was if I picked you up."

"But—"

"Get moving."

Once we found the van, even Bosko cringed.

It was parked diagonally and took up almost three spaces. I wouldn't have thought it was possible if I hadn't seen it myself.

"Whoa," Bosko said, under his breath.

"Just wait," I told him. "It gets worse."

And it did.

When Wendy wasn't slamming the brakes on the way home, she was swerving toward the double line, and just when I thought I wouldn't survive the ride, she pulled out her cell phone.

"What are you doing?" I gasped.

"What does it look like?"

"You're not allowed to call people when you're driving."

"I'm not going to," she said.

I let out the breath I was holding. "Good."

"I'm sending a quick text."

"What?" I choked.

"Isn't that illegal?" Bosko asked, with a gulp.

I'd never seen him scared before, and it would have been funny if I hadn't been terrified, myself.

"What are you, a hall monitor?" she sneered.

I stared at her. "Okay, that doesn't even make sense."

"Shut up, Nugget," she snapped, steering with one hand while she typed letters with the other.

"You're going to kill us," I told her.

"Yeah, right," she said.

"Stop, Wendy," I said, seeing the traffic slowing down in front of us.

"I'm almost done."

"No, I mean stop!" I shouted.

The car in front of us wasn't moving.

But we were.

Fast.

There was a huge crunch and I was thrown forward, hard. I was glad I was wearing my seatbelt, because otherwise I would have been hurled in the air for a couple of blocks, probably all the way into a booth at KFC.

When all the noise stopped, we didn't say anything for a moment. We just stared at the car in front of us.

"No way," Wendy whispered, covering her mouth with her hand. "No way did that just happen."

"Are you okay?" Bosko asked.

Even he looked kind of shaken up.

"*No way did that just happen*," she said again.

"I heard you the first time, and it did," I told her. I watched the driver in front of us get out of his car and check for damage.

He didn't have to look very hard.

He frowned and signalled for Wendy to get out of the car.

My sister shook her head and didn't move. "This can't be happening," she mumbled. "They're going to kill me."

"Who?" I asked, imagining the other guy's car was loaded with gangsters or bloodthirsty zombies.

"Mum and Dad," she whispered.

"Well, duh. How many times have they told you not to use your stupid cell phone while you're driving?"

She dropped her hand from her mouth and turned to face me. "Don't you dare tell them."

"They're gonna know," I told her. "Unless you can do some serious body work in the next hour or so."

"It might not be that bad," Bosko said, jumping out of the car to take a look.

When Wendy saw him cringe, I thought she might cry.

"They won't make you pay for it," I told her.

"Shut up, Nugget."

"They won't," I insisted. "Dad's an insurance guy, for crying out loud."

She held up a hand. "Just stop talking."

I looked out the front window and saw either smoke or steam blowing out from under the hood.

My sister's eyes were huge. "Is it going to blow up?"

I stared at her. "This isn't an action movie, Wendy."

But it started to seem like one when I saw the flashing lights of two police cars heading our way.

"The police?" she whispered.

"Mum and Dad are going to kill you," I finished for her.

One of the policemen came to Wendy's window and when he signalled for her to roll it down, she shook her head and looked away.

"I don't think that will work," I told her.

"Maybe we can just drive to a garage and I can pay for it out of my savings. Maybe Mum and Dad don't have to know."

"What are you, five?" I asked. "That's the kind of plan Kenny would come up with."

"You're not helping, Nugget. Can you please just be quiet?"

The policeman rapped his knuckles against the glass and I swore Wendy jumped about a foot. And that was with her seatbelt on.

"Just get out of the car and deal with it," I told her.

She closed her eyes for a second, then unlocked the door and climbed out to talk to the police. I followed her, wondering if they'd take her to the station.

That would be pretty awesome. I'd only been there once, for a field trip in grade two.

Bosko and I sat on the curb while Wendy and the other driver told the police what had happened. No one asked us anything, even though we'd been closer to the action than anyone. We were perfect eyewitnesses, but nobody cared.

When it turned out that Mum's van was too messed up to drive, and would have to be towed away, Wendy came and sat with us. That's when she really did start crying.

Bosko saw an opportunity and tried to put his arm around her.

She punched him in the neck.

Hard.

I watched her biting her lip as she dialed our home number and told Mum where she was. I couldn't think of another time when Wendy had been in big trouble. Sure, my parents had talked to her about her attitude every now and then, but she'd never done anything seriously wrong.

And this was seriously wrong.

And seriously stupid.

It was going to be interesting.

"Wanna get started on the Math?" I asked Bosko.

"I guess we could," he said, glancing at Wendy to make sure she wasn't suddenly going to change her mind and leap into his arms.

She wasn't. I grabbed my textbook out of the van and we got to work while Wendy stared off into the distance, still biting her lip.

When my parents showed up and saw their almost-new van smashed up, they looked madder than I'd ever seen them.

"What happened?" Mum asked.

Wendy fiddled with the zipper on her hoodie. "I was, uh . . ."

"Texting," the guy she hit told them.

"What?" Mum gasped, staring at my sister. "You've got to be kidding."

Wendy shook her head. "I'm sorry."

"You're sorry?" Mum laughed, but in kind of a crazy way. "You're *sorry*?"

"Yeah," she said quietly.

"You're paying the deductible," Mum said. "I don't care how you do it or how long it takes."

"And this looks like the end of driving for a while," Dad added.

"Not to mention leaving the house," Mum said.

"What?" Wendy gasped. "Are you serious?"

"Absolutely," Dad told her. "Grounded."

It was kind of cool to watch my parents tag team somebody else for a change.

"School and volleyball," Mum said. "That's it."

"But Shane—"

"You're not seeing Shane," Mum said.

"What?" Wendy almost choked on the word.

Bosko started to grin like he'd won the freakin' Stanley Cup.

While we were all making a scene, a big, black SUV pulled up next to us. When the driver jumped out, he had a neck like a tree stump and I immediately knew who he was.

It had to be Mr. Bosko.

"What's going on here?" he asked. "You okay, son?"

Eddie nodded. "Sure."

Mr. Bosko spun around to face Dad. "You should count your lucky stars that he's okay. This kid is a *prodigy*. Do you know what that means?" he asked, then looked from Wendy (gnawing on a fingernail) to me (mouth hanging open like a flounder) and back again before shaking his head and muttering, "Of course you don't."

"Look, I'm—"

"The hockey coach," he said, with a sneer. "I know exactly who you are."

"Gord McDonald," Dad said, offering his hand for a shake.

"Give me a break," Mr. Bosko said, turning away. "Eddie, get in the car."

"But—"

"*Now*," he said, following his son to the SUV.

I had a sneaking suspicion I wouldn't be seeing Bosko next practice.

And that meant the McDonald family had managed to lose three players for the Cougars.

It was quite the record.

Chapter Fifteen

When I came home on Tuesday, I was sick of everything. I'd had a bad day at school, I was sure we'd be down three players at the next game and I was just plain sick of everything.

As soon as I walked in the door, I threw my backpack into the mudroom. Hard.

"Whoa!" Mum said, when I got to the kitchen. "What was that?"

"Nothing."

"It was a pretty loud nothing," she said, raising an eyebrow at me.

"It was my backpack, okay?"

"No," she said, frowning. "Not okay at all, Nugget. This isn't the place to throw things."

"There's nothing breakable in it," I told her, starting toward the fridge.

"That's not the point," she said, leaning against the door so I couldn't open it.

I gave the handle a huge tug, but she was heavier than she looked. "What?" I snapped.

"First, pick up your bag, then we'll talk about *what*."

I gritted my teeth and went back into the mudroom, got the bag and hung it on a hook.

"No homework today?" Mum asked.

"Yes, I have homework," I muttered. I always had homework. That was one more thing I was sick of.

"Then the bag is probably going upstairs with you, don't you think?"

I stared at her. "Whatever."

"Nugget, what's going on?" she asked, carrying a cup of coffee over to the table and sitting down.

"Nothing."

"I find that impossible to believe. Is it Math?"

"No." Yes, but that was only a small part of it.

"English?"

"No."

"Social Studies?"

"*No*. Look, it's not school at all, okay?"

It was Mum's turn to stare. "Then what is it?"

"Hockey," I mumbled.

"You're going to have to speak up."

"It's hockey, okay?" I snapped.

"Let's watch the tone, young man."

I took a deep breath. "Sorry. I'm just upset."

"About hockey," Mum said, looking surprised.

I nodded. "Pretty much."

"What's going on? Is it one of the other guys? Bosko?"

"No."

"Kenny?"

"No."

"Colin?"

"No, Mum. Can you stop trying to guess?"

"Well, yes. If you tell me."

I took a deep breath. "It's Dad."

"Dad?" she paused for a second. "Is he being too hard on you? Because if he is, it's only because he wants you to play well and—"

"He's not being too hard on me."

"Then what is it?"

"It's everything," I said, slumping into a chair. "It started with practice, when he wanted to do all the weird drills and running and everything."

"He is the coach for now, honey. He can't let you guys slack off."

"I know. It's just that since he moved everyone into different positions—"

"To strengthen the team, on a part-time basis," she interrupted. "He explained that to both of us."

"Well, the guys don't like it. The parents don't like it. I don't even like it."

"When you say 'it,' do you mean the changes, or Dad as a coach?"

I bit my lip. "I don't even know, Mum. Of course I love Dad, but he's kind of tearing the team apart."

"Then what he's trying to do isn't really coming across. Have you talked to him about it?"

"I can't," I shrugged.

"Why not?"

"Because I can tell he likes coaching and—"

"You don't want to hurt his feelings," she said, with a nod.

"No, I don't."

"Do you want me to talk to him?"

Part of me wanted her to, but I didn't think that would solve anything either. "No."

"Well, can you talk to the guys?"

"I've tried, but like I said, they hate the drills and the running and they think he's favouring me and—"

"Is he?"

I shrugged again, thinking about keeping my position. "Kind of."

Mum shook her head. "I don't know what to tell you, kiddo. You don't want to talk to him, you don't want *me* to talk to him, you don't want to talk to the guys—"

"I know," I sighed.

"I'd love to help, but you've turned down every suggestion I've made." Mum shrugged. "It looks like you're on your own on this one."

Great.

* * *

"Dad?" I said, sitting down next to him on the couch after dinner. "Can I talk to you?"

"Sure," he said, folding up his newspaper and putting it on the coffee table. "What's up?"

"I think we might have lost Kenny, Colin and maybe Bosko."

He nodded. "It's kind of looking that way."

"Uh-huh." I nodded too. "And that doesn't leave us with a ton of guys."

He smiled. "I don't think we've lost them for good, Nugget."

"But if they don't come back—"

"Of course they'll come back. And even if they didn't, we'd still have a full roster. We can get some bodies up off the bench."

Great. Tim and Curtis. *That* would really help.

"But when the guys see we're down all these players—"

"What are you getting at here, Nugget?"

I took a deep breath. "We need to scrimmage."

"Look, changing things up can mean a tough adjustment, but—"

"Dad, we seriously *need* to get back to normal before everybody quits the team."

He looked surprised. "Who's quitting the team?"

I sighed. "I don't know."

"I'm not following you."

"I just don't know why you have to be so stubborn about doing things your way."

Dad shook his head. "Nugget, this is the first time I've been out on the ice in years. This is my chance to make a difference, to use all the skills that have been buried for all this time."

"You can still do that without making everyone mad."

He rubbed his forehead. "I wish the players, the parents and even Coach O'Neal would let me do this my way. It's for the good of the team. I'm not trying to sabotage the season, for crying out loud."

"The guys don't know that," I told him. "Look, Dad. They think hockey is supposed to be fun all the time. They aren't like me and Bosko."

"You and Bosko?"

"Yeah. The other guys don't get that it takes a lot more work to make it to the NHL than to make it on the island."

"Ah, the NHL," Dad nodded. "Maybe they don't."

"They just want to get out there and play the game. Like, now."

"Yes, but—"

"Dad, if you don't start doing stuff like Coach O'Neal does, they aren't going to want to come at all."

Dad leaned back against the cushions. "I'm just trying to prepare them for a great season."

"And they just want to *play*. Please Dad."

He stroked his chin. "Let me think about it, okay?"

"Sure," I said.

But I wasn't sure at all.

* * *

Luckily, I was wrong about Bosko skipping Wednesday's practice, and when I saw him in the locker room, I couldn't help smiling with relief.

"I didn't think you'd be here," I said, as I dropped my bag on the bench.

We were both early, so none of the other guys were there yet, which was cool.

"Why not?" he asked, pulling an old Flames jersey over his head.

"I don't know. Your dad seemed pretty mad yesterday and—"

Bosko shrugged. "He has a pretty short fuse. Like me lately, I guess."

"He seems pretty—"

"Loud? Angry? Unreasonable?"

"Well, yeah."

"That's just the way he is. He gets mad about stuff, then it blows over when he finds something else to get mad about."

"I thought he was going to say something to my dad about you playing centre."

Bosko shook his head. "I doubt it. But I might."

Great. Another argument, coming up.

"You know, Dad's not trying to—"

"I don't mean today, Nugget. I listened to what you said

and I'll see how things go at the game on Saturday." He paused for a second or two. "So, is he going to try *you* out in a new position?"

"I don't know," I said.

In fact, I had no idea what he was going to do about anything.

I checked the clock and had a weird feeling that the whole team was going to pull a no-show.

Maybe I'd waited too long to talk to Dad.

But at that moment Patrick Chen walked into the locker room. I was happy to see him, but he didn't look happy to see me.

"How's it going?" I asked.

"Fine," he said, dumping his bag.

"Ready for Saturday's game?"

"I guess so," he said, unzipping it.

"What's wrong?" I asked him.

"With you?"

"No, with you," I said, confused.

"I don't know, Nugget. I thought we were solid teammates, you know?"

"Yeah," I said, feeling my stomach sink.

"So why was I the only one standing up for your dad last practice?"

"What?" Bosko asked, raising an eyebrow at me.

"Nothing," I told him.

"He backed Colin and Jeff up when they were complaining about his dad."

"Are you kidding?" Bosko asked.

"Look, I was just—"

"Then as soon as Colin and Kenny left, him and Jeff acted like it never happened," Patrick said, glaring at me.

"We're supposed to be a team, you know?"

"I know," I sighed. "I'm sorry, okay? I made a bad choice."

"No doubt," he grunted, as he started digging in his bag.

"You think Colin and Kenny will show up today?" I asked.

"No idea," Patrick shrugged.

"They'd better," Bosko said.

"Better what?" Jeff asked, as he entered the locker room.

"Show up for practice," I said. "Colin and Kenny."

Patrick spoke up again. "I don't think their dads should have acted all tough with your dad like that."

"Me neither," I sighed.

"He handled it, though," Patrick said. "I liked what he said about how they should have volunteered to coach if they were going to complain about it."

"If they don't show up, it's their loss," Jeff said.

And probably ours on Saturday.

"What do the other guys think?" I asked. "Are they going to show?"

"Who cares?" Bosko asked me.

"I do. If they don't come to practice, they don't play on Saturday. And if we don't have enough guys, we don't play either."

"Do you actually think those goofs will miss out on the season?" Bosko asked, with a snort.

"I don't know," I shrugged. Everyone had been so split on things lately, I couldn't guess what they would do.

"No way," Patrick said. "They won't miss out."

Bedhead McCafferty showed up with one of the bench-warmers and squinted at us, like he just woke up. "Are we playing today?" he asked.

"It's Wednesday," I told him. "Practice."

"I know," he sighed. "I meant are we hitting the ice today?"

"I think so," I told him.

Dad hadn't said anything about leaving skates at home when we'd left that morning.

"Well, I'm getting my gear on," Bedhead said, pulling his shoulder pads out of his bag.

I did the same, and as each of the guys came in, I waited for somebody to say something about the scene with Colin and Kenny's dads, but no one did.

I couldn't stop wishing that Dad's coaching had turned out the way I'd expected it to, where he was the hero and the Cougars played better then ever before.

I knew it wasn't totally his fault that things were all messed up, but why hadn't he just stuck to the kind of practice we were used to? Why did he have to do his own thing?

Patrick finished lacing up his skates and looked around the room. "No Colin and no Kenny," he said.

Great. We'd definitely be down two guys for Saturday's game.

And everyone would blame Dad.

Just then, Kenny walked into the locker room and everybody just stared.

I watched out of the corner of my eye as he started unloading his bag.

"Ken," Bosko said, nodding at him as he walked by on his way to the rink.

"Hey," he said, quietly, but didn't turn around.

I waited for a couple of minutes, before finally saying, "I didn't think you'd show up."

The rest of the guys turned to look at Kenny.

"Yeah, well, I wasn't supposed to," he said.

"What do you mean?" I asked.

He shrugged. "My dad doesn't know I'm here. I mean, my mum drove me, but he was still sleeping when we left."

"Will he be mad?" I asked.

"Probably," Kenny shrugged. "But I'm mad too."

"At my dad?" I asked.

Kenny looked surprised. "No, at mine."

What?

"How come?"

He stared at me for a couple of seconds. "Because he totally embarrassed me, Nugget. Geez, coming down here to chew out my coach?"

My coach.

It was the first time I'd heard any of the guys call Dad that.

"I thought you didn't like him," I said.

"What? Of course I like him. I just don't like running and all that. I like being on the ice."

"I like him, too," Patrick said. "Coach McDonald knows more about hockey than any of the other dads."

I nodded, surprised. "It just seemed like everybody hated him."

"No way," Bedhead said. "He's cool."

"It definitely stunk when we lost to the Eagles," Jeff said.

"But it rocked when we beat Nanaimo," Patrick added.

"No doubt," Kenny said. "That was our highest-scoring game ever."

I was totally relieved that the team wasn't falling apart. Could it be true that no one hated Dad?

Then I remembered something.

"What about Colin?" I asked.

"Like I said, he's a no-show." Patrick shook his head.

"Dumb," Bedhead added. "That means he can't play on Saturday. Coach O'Neal's rules."

"Coach's rules," Patrick agreed and the rest of the guys nodded.

"What if he quits the team?" I asked, quietly.

"He won't, Nugget," Bedhead said. "I know he gave Coach a hard time, but I don't think he wanted to leave when his dad made him."

I was still worried.

Colin was a really good player and, like the rest of the guys on the team, he was my friend. It would totally stink if he left the Cougars.

What if he ended up on a different team, and we had to play against him? How lame would that be?

"Are we practising, or what?" Jeff asked.

"Practising," a few of us answered and headed out to the rink.

When we got there, I was relieved to see Dad setting cones out on the ice.

Just like Coach O'Neal.

Despite everything that was happening, it felt really good to get onto that perfectly smooth, shiny rink. It seemed like I hadn't skated for weeks, but it had only been a couple of days.

I started to smile as I stepped onto the ice to warm up. My blades scraped the surface, carving it up as I headed for the far goal. I built up speed and the cold air filled up my lungs.

Kenny caught up with me, panting a little. "Hey, Nugget."

"Hey."

"I just wanted to say I'm sorry."

"It's okay."

"No, I mean, not just for my dad being like that. I was kind of a jerk about your dad coaching, and I'm sorry."

"Thanks, Kenny."

"We're cool?" he asked.

"Always," I told him, as we reached the net. "Race you back," I said, taking off fast.

I smiled as I skated, glad that some things were getting back to normal.

When he was ready to get started, Dad blew his whistle and called us to centre ice.

"Okay, guys. Today we're going to do some of Coach O'Neal's drills."

"And scrimmage?" I asked, hopefully.

"And scrimmage," Dad said, with a nod. "Look, guys. I realize I threw you into kind of a different style of practice, and I know it's been tough to adapt."

Awesome. That was the perfect thing to say.

He took a breath. "That said, the plyometrics and running are an important part of training."

Uh-oh. Don't let things go sideways.

"But so is ice time," he said, glancing at me.

Whew!

"From now on, we'll do a mixture of strength training drills and ice time on Mondays, then all ice on Wednesdays. How does that sound?"

"Cool," Kenny said.

I was glad he was the first one to speak up, and even more glad when the rest of the guys followed suit.

"Great," Dad said. "Now let's get down to business."

And he meant it.

The first thing we did was skate a few warm-up laps and, as usual, I worked to keep pace with Bosko. I don't know what he had for breakfast, but the giant had a full tank going for him. As we lapped Kenny and Bedhead for the second time, I glanced over and saw that he hadn't even broken a sweat.

I had, though. I could taste the salt on my lips and I was starting to get a cramp in my side.

In the middle of the laps, Mulligan showed up. He'd never been to any of our practices before, so it was kind of weird. Especially when he walked out to centre ice for a long, quiet talk with Dad. It was long enough that I wondered if Dad had forgotten we were all still skating, waiting for him to blow the whistle. I couldn't hear what they were saying, but I could tell they weren't arguing. That was a relief.

When Dad finally blew the whistle to stop, I was almost a full metre ahead of Bosko.

Nice!

"Let's get some line drills going," Dad said.

I still needed to catch my breath, but I got into position with everybody else, anyway.

I skated hard and fast, but this time I couldn't keep up with Bosko. It was down to the line and back, over and over again, to the point that my legs were burning almost as much as my lungs.

When we finally finished the drill, I watched as Dad explained the next one, waving his arms around to help describe what we were supposed to do.

He looked totally happy.

And so was I.

Chapter Sixteen

On Saturday, we had to travel to Sooke. That would have been cool, but the McDonald family minivan was still in the shop, and Mum needed Dad's car to visit an old friend in Comox.

"I guess we're bumming a ride," I said. "Should I call Kenny?"

Dad frowned. "The Cavanaughs? I don't know."

"I'm sure his dad has calmed down by now." I wasn't really sure at all, but I knew they'd have room in their van.

Dad thought about it for a second or two. "Okay, let's ask if we can carpool."

It turned out that the price for a ride was an earful from Mr. Cavanaugh.

He and Dad sat in the front seats, while Kenny and I listened from the back. It started out okay.

"Look, Gord, I know I didn't handle things too well at practice. I'd like to apologize."

"I appreciate that, Glen," Dad said, and at that moment, it seemed like things would be nice and smooth for the drive.

But Mr. Cavanaugh wasn't finished.

"I just wish you'd stuck to O'Neal's game plan."

"Sure," Dad said, glancing at me in the mirror.

"Here we go," Kenny whispered.

"All this jumping up and down, Gord? What's that really doing for the boys?"

"Well, it's building up their—"

"I mean, we're all paying for this ice time, and it's just going to waste."

"It's not going to waste, Glen. We're doing a balanced series of—"

"We want to get to the playoffs this year."

Dad cleared his throat. "We get to the playoffs every year, and this one won't be an exception."

"I heard Coach is healing up really nicely."

"So did I."

"Here's hoping," Mr. Cavanaugh said, quietly.

I saw the muscles in Dad's jaw pulsing and knew he was ticked off. And I was too.

Of course we all wanted Coach O'Neal to come back soon, but Mr. Cavanaugh didn't have to insult Dad in the meantime.

"Sorry," Kenny whispered.

I just shook my head. "It's okay," I told him, even though it wasn't.

After a few more minutes, the dads seemed to be finished talking to each other, especially when Mr. Cavanaugh tuned in to PUCK radio and turned it up loud.

The drive was kind of a long one, but it went by pretty fast while we listened to the Blues play the Red Wings.

It probably went by a lot slower for Kenny, who looked like he might cry during the third period, when his beloved

Red Wings were getting seriously smoked.

"You've got to start backing the Canucks," I told him, when the Blues scored yet another goal.

"Nah," he said. "Detroit will be my team until I'm dead."

"It's games like this that'll kill you," I laughed.

"Yeah, well they're eight and two so far this season, so they kind of left your Canucks in the dust."

"Are you going to come over when Detroit and Vancouver play in a couple of weeks?" I asked him.

"No doubt."

"We'll see who's on top then," I warned him.

"Yeah, we will."

"You know you can't wear any of your team gear for that game, right?" I said, elbowing him.

"Try to stop me," he said, laughing and elbowing me back.

It was really cool that me and Kenny were back to normal.

When we finally made it to the Sooke rink, my whole body was stiff from being stuck in the van. Me and Kenny both yawned and stretched while Mr. Cavanaugh unlocked the back door then passed us our bags.

I saw some of the other guys in the parking lot. Mrs. Chen had painted "Go Cougars" all over her windows in our team colours, which was awesome. I'd have to talk Mum into doing that for our next away game. Maybe everyone could do it, and we'd come into town like a parade.

A victory parade, before the game had even started.

Nice!

Jeff was shovelling a hot dog down his throat, a sight

that would have totally freaked Mum out. The only hot dogs allowed in our house were made of tofu.

I know. Gross.

Bedhead looked like he'd slept the whole way there, and I just hoped he managed to get all the crusty junk out of his eyes by the time the game started.

Even more gross.

"We're gonna take these guys down," Jeff said.

"They won't even know what hit them," Patrick agreed.

I sure hoped they were right.

The Cougars needed a big win.

But more than that, Dad needed one.

* * *

When we walked inside the rink, Colin and his dad were standing there, waiting for us.

"He skipped practice," Kenny whispered. "He can't play, can he?"

I shook my head. "Not by Coach O'Neal's rules."

"What's he wearing his uniform for?" Patrick asked me.

"No idea," I said, shrugging.

I was hoping Mr. Bechter wasn't going to make a big scene.

"Colin," Dad said, nodding at him. "Mr. Bechter."

Colin's dad cleared his throat. "My boy's ready to play."

I held my breath, waiting to see what Dad would do.

"I'm afraid that won't be today," he said.

"Excuse me?" Mr. Bechter asked, his whole body already tensing up.

"I'm sorry, but if you skip the practice before the game, you don't play." Dad looked at Colin. "You know that, don't you, son?"

Colin gave him the tiniest nod I'd ever seen. In fact, I wasn't even sure I had seen it.

"But we need him," Jeff said.

He was right, and I couldn't help thinking that if Dad hadn't been the one coaching at last week's game, none of this would be happening. Colin would have been at practice, as usual, and everything would be just fine.

When I looked around at the other guys' faces, I could tell they were thinking the same thing.

"We'll get by," Dad told him. "Just like we got by at practice."

Mr. Bechter crossed his arms. "He was sick."

Kenny nudged me. "No he wasn't," he whispered.

"I know," I whispered back, shocked that Mr. Bechter would stand there and lie to all of us.

"This is only a game, Mr. Bechter," Dad said. "But it's also a tool to teach these kids about teamwork, dedication, and doing the right thing. Colin," Dad looked right at him. "Were you sick?"

"Of course he was," Mr. Bechter snapped. "I just told you that."

"I'm not asking you," Dad said, then looked at Colin again. "Were you sick?"

"What's he supposed to do?" Kenny whispered. "His dad will freak if he tells the truth."

"But the guys will freak if he lies to our faces."

Colin looked at his dad, then his eyes drifted from Bedhead to Jeff, then Patrick, Chris, Bosko, Kenny and me.

We all knew the truth.

But was he going say it?

"Colin," Dad said again. "Did you miss practice because you were sick?"

"No," he said, quietly.

Whew!

I saw that Patrick and Jeff were both nodding, like they knew it had been tough for Colin to go against what his dad was saying.

We all knew it.

Kenny whispered, "Right on."

"I appreciate your honesty," Dad said, patting Colin on the back. "I'd like you to stay for the game and cheer your teammates on from the bench, if that's okay with you."

Colin looked at his dad, who was frowning. "Can I?"

Mr. Bechter stared at him for a few seconds. "I'm not staying."

I couldn't believe it! They'd driven all the way to Sooke and he wasn't going to let Colin watch the game?

Colin looked at Dad and shrugged like he was sorry.

But what else could he do?

"We can give you a ride home," Kenny offered.

Mr. Bechter turned to stare at him.

"That's right," Mr. Cavanaugh said, firmly. "We'll take him."

I wished I'd thought of that, even though it wasn't our van. It was my turn to whisper, "Right on."

We were all in it together.

Mr. Bechter left without even saying goodbye, or wishing us luck or anything.

"Thanks, Glen," Dad said.

Mr. Cavanaugh nodded. "Thanks for sticking to your guns. The 'no practice, no game' rule is there for a reason."

I was hoping that Dad would let Colin play anyway, since it wasn't his fault that he didn't make it to practice. But he didn't.

The rules were the rules.

"You boys better get ready," Dad said. "The locker room is that way."

Me and the rest of the guys headed down the hallway while Colin stood next to Dad and Mr. Cavanaugh.

I waved him over. "Come on, Colin," I said. "You're not playing, but we still need you."

"Yeah," Patrick called over his shoulder, "You're with us."

Colin grinned and followed us down the hallway. His smile got even bigger when Bosko gave him a high five.

When we got to the locker room, the Seagulls had left a nice little welcome note, taped to one of the lockers.

It said: COUGARS 4, EAGLES 5. SEE YOU ON THE ICE, LOSERS. HA HA.

"Yeah, really funny," Jeff muttered, tearing it down and dumping it in the garbage.

"They're gonna be talking trash," Bedhead said. "And after our last game, you can't blame them."

"I'm really sorry I'm not playing," Colin said, quietly. "This could be a tough game and I'm letting you down."

"It's not your fault," I told him and the others nodded.

"I don't want to hear a bunch of garbage from these guys," Jeff said.

"Well, the whole league probably knows the Eagles crushed us," Kenny said.

"What they don't know is that we weren't playing our usual positions," Jeff said.

"Is Coach keeping everyone in their new spots?" Colin asked me.

Uh-oh.

"I think so," I nodded.

"Except you," Kenny said, and I shot him a dirty look.

Nuts! Why bother bringing that up when we were starting to feel like a real team again?

"And me," Patrick said. "I'm still defense."

Thank you!

As much as I loved playing right wing, part of me was still hoping Dad would put me somewhere else instead of giving me the special treatment.

"So, let's think of the Eagles game as a practice run," Colin said. "Now everybody knows what they're doing. Everyone's got the new positions figured out, right?"

I liked the fact that he was ready to boost us up, even though he couldn't play.

"I made my brother take shots on me all week," Bedhead said. "My sister, too."

I smiled.

"I've been working on my shooting," Kenny said.

"Cool," I nodded.

"I think I've got a handle on centre now," Bosko added, as we headed out to the rink.

And did he ever!

The Seagulls had come prepared, with a lot of attitude and what felt like some extra elbows, but that was okay.

We were prepared, too.

After last week's humiliation and all the drama over practice, we were just plain ready to play.

And to win, of course.

From the second the puck was dropped, Bosko played the game of his life. In fact, we all did.

Our passing was awesome, and no one hesitated to share the puck. We only took shots when the time was right, and whenever a Seagull started talking trash, it ended with a quick slam against the boards.

It was really cool to see everyone play their new positions like they'd been playing them all along. And I guess that's what Dad was aiming for. If we all mastered more than one position, we'd be a stronger team than ever.

We'd be full-on dangerous.

I had a breakaway just a couple of minutes into the second period, with two goons right on my tail. There was nothing but a goalie to stop me, and I could hear the home crowd getting desperate for the Seagulls to steal the puck.

But they couldn't.

"Go for it!" Kenny shouted, from way behind me.

I didn't need instructions. It was the kind of moment I was built for.

"Shoot!" Patrick shouted, as I got nice and close to the net.

"You stink!" one of the Seagulls called out.

But the voice I heard the clearest was Dad's, yelling, "Let it rip, Nugget!"

I lined up the puck, with the goons panting behind me. Before they had a chance to catch up, I whaled on it.

I felt the stick make contact, then watched it go airborne, heading right toward the sweet spot.

And then?

The stupid goalie deflected it!

Right at Bosko, who was ready, like he always was.

He took a crack at the puck and it sailed right into the lower corner of the net while the goalie was still adjusting his mask.

"Yes!" I shouted, happy he scored but wishing the goal was mine.

"Nugget's still up by three," Patrick called out from the bench.

"We'll see about that," Bosko called back with a laugh.

All the guys skated up to Bosko and slapped his back or helmet, depending on their height.

I ended up punching his elbow.

That was as far as I could reach.

"Nice play!" Dad shouted.

The Seagulls came back pretty hard after that, and I had to admit, they made it tough to keep up.

But Bosko was shooting like Gretzky.

Exactly what I'd been afraid of.

"We're tied, Nugget," he said with a smile at the end of the second period. "You know I'm gonna win." He smiled. "Playing centre might just put me over the top."

I thought about how tricky it had been to convince him that the position switch was a good idea. And how much it stunk when the team split up into sides.

The Cougars were about winning games. It was as simple as that.

Did it really matter who scored the most goals?

Well, of course it did.

And Bosko was probably right about coming out on top.

But there had to be another way I could beat him.

"I'll probably have the most assists," I told him.

"Is that a challenge?" he asked, with a laugh.

"Oh, yeah." I smiled back at him. As long as the team was working together, a little friendly competition couldn't hurt.

* * *

As the game went on, the Seagulls fans were easy to spot in the crowd, mostly because they were all wearing the light blue and white team colours.

But they were also easy to spot because they were getting totally mad every time we scored.

Which was a lot.

Bedhead still seemed a little freaked out in the net, but the practice at home had definitely helped. He was managing to not only stay alert, but make saves.

Like, *seven* during the third period.

"You're doing awesome," I told him, when Dad called a time-out. "Maybe even better than Chris."

"Seriously?" he asked.

I nodded. "You're quick."

"And fearless," Patrick added.

"And awake," Jeff laughed.

When the clock finally ran out, we had won the game, 11–4.

"So," Colin said, when we all piled into the Cavanaughs' van for the drive home. "What position am I going to play in the next game, Coach?"

I held my breath, waiting for Dad to say he had to stay a defenseman.

Would Colin point out that I never had to switch?

Why didn't Dad just make me try something new, so it wouldn't be an issue?

"I'm thinking we should move you back up to the front line," Dad said.

I let out the breath I'd been holding.

"Sweet," Colin said, leaning back in his seat.

And it *was* swect. We won the game, the team was united, and we were going to kick some serious butt against Courtenay next Saturday.

Things were finally back on track.

Chapter Seventeen

On Sunday, I went for a jog with Dad in the morning, which was something we'd never done before. It was nice and quiet, and I really liked hanging with him. So much had happened in the past few weeks, it was cool to just be alone together.

"I'm glad everything's kind of settled down," I told him, after we'd been at it for a few minutes.

"What? Oh, you mean the Cougars?"

"Yeah, things were getting kind of weird, you know?"

"I do know," Dad said, in between breaths.

"It's been pretty cool having you as a coach, Dad," I told him.

"All the time?" he asked, chuckling.

I thought about how to answer. "Maybe not every second of it, but most of the time."

"I've enjoyed it, too," he said. "I really think this could be one of your best seasons."

We jogged in silence for a couple of minutes.

"Is it pretty fun, coaching?" I asked.

He was quiet for a second. "There have been some surprises along the way, so it hasn't been exactly what I expected."

Me neither.

"But it's been great to get out on the ice again," he added.

We ran for about half an hour, then headed back to the house.

"Hey Dad," I said, wanting to get to the bottom of something that had been bugging me. "Why did you let me keep my position and move Bosko?"

I really didn't want to hear that the guys were right and he was playing favourites.

But then he said something even worse.

"He's a more adaptable player," he said, with a shrug.

"What?" I choked.

"You're both great at right wing, Nugget. That goes without saying."

"Then why are you saying it?" I asked.

"Look, you two have very different styles. You like a steady game plan, without a lot of shake-ups, while Bosko flies by the seat of his pants a bit."

I didn't like the sound of that at all.

"So, you're saying he's better."

"No. I'm saying he's more open to change than you are, and that's what backing up a position is all about. I figured it would take less time for him to learn a new position, and that's true of all the guys I moved."

"So, he's smarter," I muttered. "Like we didn't already know that."

"It's got nothing to do with who's smarter or better, son. This way, we got two of the Cougars' top players on the ice at the same time by having just one of them switch positions."

I thought about it for a minute.

It didn't sound so bad when he put it that way.

* * *

When we got home, Mum had left a note, saying she was grocery shopping. Wendy was on the phone in the kitchen.

Surprise, surprise.

Dad signalled for her to hang up, but she only glanced at him for a second and kept talking.

Bad idea, considering she was grounded.

"Off the phone," Dad told her.

"What?" she mouthed. She tried to look confused, but she was a terrible actress.

"Hang up the phone, Wendy."

"I'm in the middle of—"

"Now," he said, and she saw that he meant business.

"Fine," she snapped. "Look, I have to go." She hung up and glared at Dad. "I can't believe you."

"Hey," he shrugged. "It's all part of the punishment."

"I seriously hate this family," she shouted, running upstairs.

Dad sighed, then looked at me and smiled. "I remember how excited Mum and I were when she said her first word. And look at us now." He laughed and shook his head. "Let's get some breakfast going, Nugget."

"How about waffles?" I asked.

"Can you make them?"

"No. Can you?"

"No. How about toast?"

"Toast always works," I told him.

I grabbed all the jams, jellies and peanut butter out of the pantry while Dad set out plates.

"Teamwork," I told him, when I dropped the bread into the toaster slots and he pushed the button.

Of course, we ended up burning it, but that was okay.

We were both willing to pretend it tasted good.

After all, sometimes we guys had to stick together.

* * *

When my alarm went off on Monday morning, I was out of bed like a shot, ready for practice.

I knew the guys would still be feeling the adrenalin rush from Saturday's win, and that made me even more anxious to get to the rink.

But when Dad and I got there, I couldn't believe what I saw.

Coach O'Neal was leaning on a cane, waiting for us.

No way!

I was excited to see him, which made me feel kind of guilty.

"Coach!" I said, giving him a high five. "I thought you were stuck in a hospital bed."

"They did some laser surgery."

"Lasers?" I asked. How cool was that?

"It turned out I'd chipped a bone in my back, so they smoothed down the sharp edges."

"But I thought you were out for ages," I said. Of course, I was happy to see him and I wanted him to come back, but what about Dad leading us to the championship?

What would happen to him?

"I guess I'll heal up pretty quick. I'm supposed to be getting some regular exercise, so I walked down here from the house this morning." He cleared his throat. "I'd heard about how things were going and figured it wouldn't hurt to check in on you guys."

"Sure," Dad said. His smile looked more like a wince and I felt sorry for him.

"That Esquimalt loss really tears at my gut," Coach O'Neal said, shaking his head.

"But we whaled on Nanaimo and Sooke," I told him, defending Dad.

Coach looked at me, then at him. "Have you got a minute to talk, Gord?"

"Sure," Dad said, looking uncomfortable.

It didn't take a genius to figure out that they wanted some privacy, so I headed for the locker room.

The whole way there, I worried that Coach was going to chew Dad out, and that he wouldn't have a chance to explain the method to his madness.

I slumped on the bench, next to my bag.

What if Coach was rushing to get better because he was freaked out about what Dad was doing? And if Coach bumped Dad back to the stands, how humiliating would that be? What if Mr. Bechter had made some kind of a formal complaint?

All of the questions were making me feel sick, but I couldn't stop them from coming.

No one had the right to put Dad down for all the work he'd done to help us.

Not even Coach O'Neal.

The more I thought about it, the madder I got.

While I was stewing, Kenny and Patrick showed up together, all excited.

"Coach O'Neal is here," Patrick told me, grinning.

"I know," I muttered.

"What's wrong?" Kenny asked.

"Nothing."

"You want him back, don't you, Nugget?" Patrick asked, dropping his bag next to mine.

"Well, duh," I said, quietly.

Of course I wanted him back, but not if it was a slap in Dad's face.

I didn't even finish dressing. Instead, I headed back out to the rink with my shoulder pads half on to see what was happening.

Ever since Dad took over, I'd felt like I was on some kind of a roller coaster (or driving with Wendy). I was up and down every day, hoping nobody was mad at anyone else, or no one's feelings were hurt, and basically worrying that the team wouldn't keep it together.

Dad had tried really hard to get us on track for the championship, and even though I didn't agree with the way he'd handled everything, I was proud of him.

Why couldn't things have worked out better?

The more I imagined what Coach might be saying, the more I thought about how I'd felt when Patrick stood up for Dad, and again when Bosko did it.

I thought about all the times Bosko had shut the guys up when they were complaining. And how he'd dragged Tim and Curtis back to centre ice when they were being so rude. How he'd dropped them at Dad's feet and threatened to go after Colin and Jeff.

I couldn't go back in time to do something then, but I had a pretty awesome opportunity to do something now.

It was my turn.

I spotted Dad and Coach in the main office and watched through the window as they talked. They didn't look like they were arguing, but I couldn't hear anything they were saying.

I unclenched my fists.

If I didn't know what was going on, was it the right time to charge in and start yelling?

Probably not.

As I watched them, I tried to figure out what I should do.

And what I should do was . . . something.

I'd spent too much time watching other people do the dirty work.

I took a deep breath and walked into the office.

Dad turned to look at me. "We're having a private conversation here, buddy."

"I know," I said, looking at him for a second, then at Coach. "I just wanted to say that my dad has done an awesome job and—"

"Jonathan," Dad warned.

"And even though we blew an easy game and we don't like plyometrics and the guys weren't getting along and I thought Dad might be crazy and Mr. Bechter probably gave you an earful already," I took a breath and tried to ignore Dad's mouth hanging open like a flounder, "and even though we've been running instead of skating and the team mums started heckling Dad—"

"Jonathan," Dad warned again.

"I just want you to know that we're a better team because of his coaching."

"I see," Coach O'Neal said, nodding slowly.

"And—"

"I think you've said enough, son," Coach O'Neal said. "Now your Dad and I need to finish our conversation."

I glanced at Dad, who just nodded.

When I left the office, I replayed what I'd said in my head and started to panic. Maybe Coach hadn't known all that stuff already. Maybe by trying to stand up for Dad, I'd actually made things worse!

Nuts!

When Dad came out a couple of minutes later, he didn't look happy. But he didn't look mad, either. In fact, he looked like I did when I was working on a tough Math problem.

Like he was thinking pretty hard.

"What's going on?" I asked him.

Dad glanced over at me, surprised I was there. "Well, you're supposed to be dressing for practice."

"I know. I meant between you and Coach."

"Nothing to worry about, Nugget."

But that only made me worry more.

Double nuts!

I'd blown everything for him!

* * *

Once the Cougars were all out on the ice, Coach O'Neal sat on the bench to watch us practise. It made me nervous for Dad, so I worked my tail off for the whole hour and I was glad to see the other guys did too.

I didn't have a chance to talk to Dad before Mrs. Cavanaugh drove me and Kenny to school, so all day I wondered what had been said in that office.

Coach's timing was crummy, considering we were winning, Dad was happy coaching the team and the guys had really come around. We were finally all on the same page, but the book was being slammed shut. Now Dad would have to go back to being just a fan, and as if that wasn't bad enough, Coach had probably criticized everything he'd done for us.

The whole situation stunk, and I couldn't stop thinking about it.

* * *

That night, when my family sat down to dinner, I hadn't even taken a bite of my chicken when I asked, "What's happening with the team, Dad?"

He scooped some green beans onto his fork. "You mean for me?"

"Yeah." I paused for a second or two. "Is Coach back for good?"

Dad nodded. "In a couple of weeks. Three, tops." He popped the beans in his mouth and started chewing.

I was disappointed to hear it, mostly because I was sure Dad's feeling were hurt. But he was covering it pretty well.

"Tell him the rest, hon," Mum said.

"The rest of what?" I asked.

"Well," Dad said, wiping his mouth with a napkin. "He liked the fact that I'd added plyometrics to your practices."

"He did?" I asked, stunned.

"Don't act so shocked," he laughed. "He said he was going to introduce that kind of training next season, but he was happy I'd gone ahead."

"*And*," Mum said, nodding for him to say more.

"And he asked me to be Assistant Coach when he gets back," Dad said, with a shrug.

A shrug, like it wasn't the coolest news on the planet!

"No way!" I shouted.

"Can you like, not yell at the table?" Wendy snapped.

I ignored her, excited that everything was suddenly turning around. All of my worrying was for nothing! Assistant Coach would be perfect. Dad could still help guide the Cougars to greatness, but Coach O'Neal would be the one who got blamed when things went wrong.

Dad wouldn't be arguing with parents or having debates about plyometrics. And best of all, he wouldn't be leaving his coaching position all embarrassed that it hadn't worked out.

I couldn't have come up with a better idea myself.

It solved everything!

But then I thought back to the look on Dad's face when he'd left Coach's office that morning. "But you weren't happy after you talked to him."

Dad nodded. "Well, it was a lot to think about."

What?

A lot to think about? I'd spent all day worrying about how he'd feel when Coach bumped him, and he'd actually been invited to stay? I mean, what was there to think about?

"What are you talking about?" I finally asked.

"Look," he said, glancing at each of us. "I gave it a lot of thought today, and I'm going to pass on the offer."

"What?" I choked. "Why?"

"Because I don't want the job," he said, with a shrug.

Another shrug, like it was no big deal to turn down an awesome opportunity!

"What do you mean?" I asked, getting frustrated. "I went in there and stood up for you and—"

"I appreciate that and—"

"You want to be Head Coach, so you can't settle for Assistant?"

Dad laughed. "I don't want to settle for anything, Nugget."

I shook my head, hoping something would start making sense.

"But sometimes you have to settle," I told him. "That's

what you've been teaching the whole team. That's why Bedhead is rocking as a goalie right now and Bosko will probably lead the league in points this season by playing part-time centre."

Dad shook his head. "I haven't been teaching you guys to settle for anything. I've been trying to help you open up to new experiences."

"*Dad.*"

Why couldn't he just take Coach up on the offer?

"I liked the idea of coaching, so I gave it a go. It turned out there were parts I loved and parts I didn't."

"But—"

"Let him finish, honey," Mum said, resting a hand on my arm.

"The best part for me was getting back on the ice, Nugget."

"So why don't you keep doing it?" I asked, totally confused.

"Because I realized coaching wasn't the best way for me to get back out there." He smiled. "Being responsible for the team involved a lot more politics than I expected."

"But—"

"I'd rather stick with being a Cougars fan."

"You can still—"

"Nugget," Mum said. "Let your dad speak."

"Yeah," my sister said, "Zip it, Nugget."

"Wendy," Mum warned.

"Mulligan and I have been talking," Dad continued, "and he wants me to play Old Timers."

"Old Timers hockey?" I asked, totally caught off guard.

So that's what they'd been talking about at centre ice that day.

That's why Dad had looked so happy.

"Yeah," he said, smiling even wider. "I never knew how much I missed playing until I dug out those old skates."

"So, you mean you're going to do it?" I asked, starting to feel kind of excited. "Like, play on a team?"

"Yes. Are you going to come and watch?"

"Definitely," I told him, grinning.

Forget coaching.

Forget assistant coaching.

My dad was going to be a hockey star again.

I'd never seen him play, but I knew he would shred the competition.

But first, he'd have to help us beat Courtenay on Saturday.

Chapter Eighteen

A couple of weeks later, my alarm went off and I jumped out of bed, ready for Coach's first practice since his surgery.

As I showered, I wondered whether Coach O'Neal would stick with the changes Dad had made to our practices and positions. It sounded like we'd still be doing plyometrics, but would he move Bosko back to full-time right wing? Chris Fullerton back to goal?

I thought Dad might have an idea about what Coach was planning, but when I got downstairs, Mum was the one making breakfast.

"Waffles?" I asked, licking my lips when I saw the plate waiting for me.

"Blueberry waffles," she said, smiling.

Right on! Toast was okay, but waffles were awesome.

And since she was back in charge of the morning routine, I couldn't help asking, "Could I maybe have a couple of brownies in my lunch?"

"They're already packed," she said, pointing at the paper bag on the counter.

Nice!

"Dad's not up?" I asked, as I spread butter into most of my waffle squares.

"Not a chance," she said, laughing. "He told me last night he was going to sleep in as long as he could."

"Cool," I said, nodding and taking a bite of my waffle. "You know, it would have been pretty cool if he'd taken the Assistant Coach job."

"Maybe," she said, shrugging. "But I think playing is going to make him happier than coaching."

I nodded. "And I'll get to watch him."

She smiled. "And he'll get to watch *you* as a fan again. No more worrying about running the show."

He'd run the show just fine, though. We'd beaten Courtenay one week and Duncan the next.

As a result, Eddie Bosko was five goals ahead of me, which drove me nuts.

But I had more assists.

"We're up against Port Alberni this weekend," I told her. "With the home advantage."

"Yeah," I said, smiling. "It's in the bag."

Mum shook her head. "It's never really in the bag, honey."

"I know," I told her, thinking about that awful Eagles game and cringing. "But the Cougars are on fire right now. It's going to take a lot more than the Port Alberni Totems to stop us."

They were a good team, but the name was as bad as the Penguins'. Totem poles were awesome to look at, but they didn't even *move*.

We were going to win on Saturday.

No doubt.

When Mum dropped me and Kenny off at the rink, we met up with Bosko, Colin and Jeff in the locker room.

"I heard Coach wanted your dad to be his assistant," Bosko said.

"He turned it down," I told them.

"It isn't because my dad was being a jerk, is it?" Colin asked.

I could tell by the look on his face that he was worried about it.

"No," I told him, shaking my head.

"It isn't because we complained about switching positions and stuff, right?" Jeff asked. "Because obviously it worked out. I mean, we smoked Courtenay and Duncan."

"Nope."

I didn't know Patrick had come in until he asked, "Why didn't your dad take the job as Assistant Coach?"

The phone tree must have been working overtime that week.

It was cool that the guys wanted Dad to stick around, but I agreed with Mum about playing being the better choice for him.

"He's going to play instead. Old Timers."

"Seriously?" Colin asked, smiling. "That's cool."

"Totally cool," Patrick agreed.

While we got dressed, Jeff asked, "So, how are you guys feeling about the Totems game this weekend?"

"Awesome," I said. "They're going down."

"I heard they've been talking trash about us, just like the Seagulls."

"Big deal," Colin said. "They won't be saying much when we skate circles around them."

"No doubt," Patrick said, smiling. "Between Bosko and Nugget playing together—"

"And Bedhead making killer saves," I said, elbowing our new goalie to wake him up. "We're winning for sure."

"Our best season ever," Kenny said, smiling.

Patrick held one gloved hand out in front of him. Jeff added his hand, then Chris, Colin, Bedhead, Bosko, the benchwarmers, all three Watson triplets and I joined in.

"Cougars on three," Patrick said.

We bumped our fists together three times, then shouted, "Cougars!"

"Now, let's do this," Colin said, as the whole team headed out to the rink.

Together.